WICKED GAMES

DAMNED MAGIC AND DIVINE FATES 2

KEL CARPENTER

Wicked Games
Kel Carpenter
Published by Kel Carpenter
Copyright © 2018, Kel Carpenter
Edited by Analisa Denny
Cover Art by Maria Spada

To all the men and women who have been mistreated or abused: it does not define you.

"Sometimes you get the best light from a burning bridge."
— Don Henley

CHAPTER 1

The stifling heat smothered my skin as fire licked at the earth around me. I padded across the endless waste-land, my arms stretched wide before me. The beast smiled down at the world on fire as blue flames spread across the land.

She enjoyed watching the humans run. The way they panted, hard and heavy, as they attempted to flee. How they would pause and look back, their faces blanching the moment they realized their feet couldn't carry them fast enough. That her rage—my rage—would consume them before they could take another step.

"Ruby!" The scream ripped me from sleep.

My eyes flew open and Moira was the first thing I saw, the glow of flickering blue flames dancing on her face as it burned all around us. Claws pricked at my upper chest as Bandit scrambled in a wild panic to climb on top of me. "Ruby!"

She straddled me, shaking me with a fervor as she let

loose a scream that could wake the dead. Our front window shattered instantly.

Shit. This wasn't the wastelands. It was my home, and Moira and Bandit had braved the flames to save it. I inhaled sharply, terror seizing my heart for them—what I could do to them—as I tried to calm the inferno. I focused on the connection and tried to force them to die out. But they only fanned higher as I panicked about my apparent lack of control.

Inside me, the beast frowned at the scene before us and snarled at Moira and Bandit for stupidly putting themselves at risk. It only took a single look from her and the fire dissipated immediately.

Well then.

"Moira," I croaked. Her scream cut off the moment the flames dispersed, leaving a thin glittering black residue that I could only assume was ash. A cold wind blew through the window, stirring up the blinds enough to let a crack of sunlight slip through and illuminate more of the scene before me.

My naked body shivered against the barren concrete where a couch and carpet used to be. My living room wasn't much more than charred remains with four walls. Piles of black dust littered the cement foundation, drifting across the room as a harsh gust of wind whipped through it. Bandit wrapped his arms around me tightly and Moira's naked body clung to mine as she gripped me in a desperate embrace. Where she had been clothed was now nothing more than a fine film of black against her pale green skin. Where everything else had been consumed, my best friend and raccoon had been spared.

"I'm sorry. I didn't mean to—" My shaky apology was interrupted by a pounding on our front door.

"One second!" Moira yelled. The loud whapping on the door ceased.

"Ruby?" Laran called. His voice drifted through the broken window with ease.

"I'm here. Just give us a second," I replied. He let out an impatient harrumph, but didn't push it. Moira jumped to her feet, pulling me up with her. The fine powdery ash covered us both, shining like granules of onyx in the low light coming from the kitchen. The large sectional couch I had been sleeping on was completely gone, as was most of the room. The fire seemed to have spread all the way to the edge of the kitchen and hallway before the beast had finally put it out.

"You really are Lucifer's kid," Moira murmured. Her seafoam green eyes had flicked to the brand in the center of my sternum.

"So it appears," I muttered back. The upside-down pentagram sat snuggly between my breasts, a thick ring of black circling it. She reached out with light green fingers to brush the brand just as another fist pounded on the door.

I felt like I jumped two feet in the air and Moira threw a harsh glare over her shoulder towards the pounding. It wouldn't hold up against Laran's fists forever.

"Come on, let's put on some clothes and greet your

males before they have a conniption." She wasn't wrong, but it felt weird hearing it out loud. *My males.* Like I owned them or something. The beast perked her head up and agreed with great vigor. They were *ours*.

I turned and walked down the hallway and into my bedroom with Bandit hot on my heels. The sweet scent of Amaryllis filled the air, but it couldn't mask the stench of charred fibers and musky raccoon. I reached over blindly to flip on the light as a massive thud sounded in my living room. I popped my head outside the bedroom.

A plume of soot and debris swirled, thick enough I couldn't make out anything but a wall of what looked like black glitter. The particles danced for a moment before descending slowly.

Laran took a sweeping glance of the room, his brow furrowing more as his gaze swept up the hallway and stopped on me.

"What happened here?" he roared. I swallowed hard, but I, nor the beast inside, was going to answer to someone who had the audacity to break the door down like an uncivilized animal after I had just told him to wait. I closed my bedroom door sharply and threw my black bathrobe on in record time. I was just tying the knot around my waist when my door creaked open.

"I would have let you in had you waited another minute for me to dress," I said sharply. My words fell on deaf ears.

"Why is there glass outside your house? What happened to the window? Why does—"

The slamming of a door cut him off abruptly. He

turned to face the she-demon behind him. Moira slipped around his hulking frame and came to stand beside me. Her own bathrobe was white and sheer, definitely sexier than anything I owned. Demons in general were very lax about clothes. I doubt she even noticed how great it made her legs look, even as black dust smudged the robe.

"Do you just storm into other people's houses without invitation all the time? Or is this bad behavior just you attempting to prove your dominance?" Moira snapped at him. His face darkened as he took a step forward, towering over us.

"That's not the question at hand, banshee," he rumbled. I wanted to facepalm myself for the pissing contest going on between the two of them.

"She could have burned down all but a single cupboard and that would still be the question. You Horsemen need to learn to respect—" He silenced her with a wave of his hand. Her jaw snapped shut as if by force.

"Hey!" I protested, whacking him in the arm with my hand. Laran raised an eyebrow at me. I didn't know whether it was surprise that I hit him, or a dare to make him stop. Either way, I didn't have to think on it long before Moira's mouth was magically unsealed.

"No talking, or I'll do it again," he said to her. If he had been talking to any other demon, they might have heeded his warning. Moira was anything but. Really, she was just bat-shit crazy.

"I'd be careful who you piss off, Laran. There's an awful lot of ghosts that like to hang around you. It would be a shame if I let slip what some of them tell me..." Her voice was sweet as sugar, but her words were nothing but a bluff. Moira never gained the ability to see the dead. As a half-banshee, she was left with very few talents outside her sonic scream. Not that Laran knew that. He gave her a leery glare that hardened the longer she smiled.

"You wouldn't dare."

"Try me," she goaded. It's a good thing I only needed a day to mope and recover. Their bickering was already driving me nuts. It was like Moira was constitutionally incapable of not picking a fight with the Horsemen about anything that involved me. If it wasn't respect, then it was stalking, or possessiveness, and she even went so far as tell them they couldn't be allowed inside because of their gender. I can't remember what day she told them that we were lesbians having hot lesbian sex and no dicks were invited. Seeing as Rysten and Allistair both knew that wasn't true...I just chose not to get into it.

"Someone want to explain to me why the living room was burned down?"

The question came from down the hall. My beast started licking her lips the moment Julian came around the corner. He looked the same as he did the night the demons came for us. His blonde hair so light it could be white, laid perfectly to one side. His skin was unmarked. Pale and without blemish. Everything about him was radiant, but his glow wasn't warm or kind. It was like an endless winter: ethereal in its beauty, but unforgiving if lost in its depths.

This was the first time I'd seen him since my drug-induced coma two nights ago. It was the first time I'd seen any of them, but for some reason, it was Julian that made me think of that night. How the lights reflected off his hair making it look violet and eerie as he carried me out. A heat crept across my skin as a faint blush stained my cheeks. After everything that happened, that was *not* what I should be feeling when I looked back at how that night played out.

"You okay?" Moira asked, returning to my side in an instant. She sent both of them a withering glare as she snaked an arm around my waist. Behind them, boots crunched on glass as someone let out a low whistle. I could only assume the other Horsemen had shown up, thankfully before I made myself look like an idiot. I was a half-succubus, not some blushing school girl that fawned over a pretty face. Julian saved me because it was his job. I would do well not to confuse the facts.

I nodded my head to silence the blood pounding in my ears and muttered, "I'm fine."

Moira didn't argue, but her arm tightened imperceptibly.

For devil's sake.

I wasn't a helpless child. I mean, I did just start a fire in my sleep. The overprotectiveness on everyone's account was more than a bit annoying, given that almost everyone who tried or had hurt me was dead. The thought was both depressing and comforting at the same time.

I shrugged off Moira's arm and pulled at the sleeves

of my bathrobe. Yesterday, I was Ruby. I ate an entire tub of ice cream and drank a pound of tea. I laid on my couch curled up in a snuggie, binge watching Netflix like I hadn't just killed someone.

Today, I woke up to my best friend screaming because I almost burned our house down.

As much as I hated to admit it, I needed to find a way to bridge that gap in my mind, because the pentagram on my chest wasn't going anywhere.

And neither were the Horsemen.

CHAPTER 2

I wish I had time to process and wrap my head around what it means to become Lucifer's daughter practically overnight. But the Four Horsemen were already standing in my room, waiting for some kind of an answer.

Unfortunately, all I had was, "Well, I kind of had an accident."

No one laughed.

Tough crowd.

"What kind of accident?" Rysten asked, pushing forward. Laran huffed, but stepped out of the doorway to let him through.

"I started a fire in the living room. I didn't realize what was happening until Moira and Bandit woke me up..." My voice trailed off as Bandit scaled the rope ladder I had made for him and flung himself into his hammock. He let out the most dramatic of sighs, like even my retelling it was too much work for him to think about. I cracked a brief smile at him, happy for the reprieve from all the strangeness of this morning.

"What were you doing when the fire started?" Rysten continued.

"Sleeping," I said. My eyes flicked back to him, only then noticing that he wasn't wearing his glamor. I chose not to comment even though the beast grinned like a fool. She preferred seeing them for what they were, not the human that Rysten could almost pose himself to be.

I didn't know if I agreed with her or not just yet, given that my thoughts were occupied by more important things. Like my lack of a living room. And that it was my fault. Not to mention that I think I was hallucinating because Bandit was wiggling his eyebrows at me... he's a raccoon...did they really even have eyebrows?

"Just sleeping?" Rysten asked slowly, his eyes squinting just a smidge. His only tell that he was worried.

"Yes."

He and Julian exchanged looks. Behind them, Allistair's gaze was frozen to my chest, but not like he was ogling. I looked down at myself to see the black fabric had parted enough between my breasts to reveal the top half of the brand that claimed my skin.

Shit.

I hastily pulled the robe tighter around my body and crossed my arms over my chest.

"When did the mark appear?" Allistair asked quietly.

"I don't really know. Sometime between getting ready Friday evening and waking up yesterday morning."

I swallowed hard, looking away. I don't know why I was so uptight about it. Maybe it was because I still haven't adjusted. Maybe it was because my brand sat seductively between my breasts. Either way, I didn't feel like discussing it or how it came about. I definitely didn't want anyone asking to see it.

"And less than thirty-six hours later you started a fire in your sleep." He didn't phrase it like a question, so I chose not to answer. "What were you dreaming about?"

I blanched, recalling those final moments before Moira woke me. Fire raged in a world consumed by flame. A world I ruled. Well...the beast and me.

I'd never had a dream quite like it before, and I wasn't keen on sharing it just yet. Given that they hadn't been pushing my return to Hell, I didn't want for them to have any reason to start again. I may be Lucifer's daughter, but I wasn't ready for that.

Not yet.

"Umm..." I drawled, extending it out like I was thinking. I scratched my chin and cocked my head. "I don't remember exactly. I woke up to Moira screaming her head off and realized the house was on fire." I shrugged, biting on my lower lip. If Allistair thought I was lying, he didn't say anything, but his eyes darkened.

"Who put the fire out?" he asked slowly. The question had a simple enough and self-explanatory answer, but the way he said it made me hesitate. Was this a test?

"I did," I replied.

"Why do you sound unsure about that?" he countered smoothly. His line of questioning was odd. Belittling, I'd say, if he didn't use that buttery soft voice of his that made me fidget uncomfortably.

"Why are you questioning me like I did something wrong?" I snapped back, stuffing my hands in my armpits to hide the shaking.

I mean, I *did* do something wrong. I set my living room on fire, but he didn't need to make me feel like a criminal about it.

"I didn't mean to upset you, Ruby. You're progressing faster than we thought you would and I'm trying to figure out how much control you have and how much is...the other one..."

The other one.

My beast.

I guess Julian did know what lurked in my eyes that night, and he must have told the others. Then again, it was around the same time the full pentagram showed up, and it was too much of a coincidence for them not to be related. Maybe the beast was as much from Lucifer as the brand on my chest. Given what I knew before that night, I had to think as much.

Someone trapped the beast and didn't want it found. Not even by me.

"How do you know about her?" I asked him warily. Julian chose that moment to step forward reservedly. If I didn't know better, I'd have thought he was afraid of me. He didn't stink of fear. I would have felt that bleeding over into me, but the cold calm that exuded from him was gentle. Soothing, even.

"She is the reason we were created. The reason you

can control the flames. Right now, she's probably agitated and feeling impatient with us for asking questions. We just need to know how much control you have, and how much she can control you. You're still new at this and we don't expect you to be perfect, but if you're in danger of transitioning soon, we can't let you out of our sight. Do you understand?" He loomed over me; dark, but not as imposing as he'd once been. Inside me, the beast smirked because she was the reason why. She liked the power she lorded over them. She liked it a lot. Almost as much as the smell of his skin and the...

I withdrew my thoughts away from her, only then realizing how close she was to the surface. She wasn't being malevolent or forcing her way for control, she simply liked them and wanted to be closer to them. She didn't care if it was me or her that got us there.

I ignored her entirely and focused on what they were asking from me.

"I'm in control, but this morning I couldn't put out the flames on my own. I panicked when Moira woke me up because I thought I had hurt her. The beast put them out once we realized what was happening." I looked away, hoping it would make her stop pushing me to go to them. She was somewhat agitated and impatient, just as Julian had guessed. Just not for the same reasons.

"Allistair's right. You are progressing faster than anticipated," Julian said, his eyes flicking back to meet Rysten's. He nodded. "We need to reevaluate the living arrangements until you're ready to return to Hell."

My mouth popped open.

That wasn't what I expected.

I glanced between the four of them, dumbfounded and shocked, but I didn't even need to say anything before Moira went off.

"Reevaluate living arrangements? Who do you think you are?" she snarled, lunging forward to stand in front of me. Devil save her.

"Her protectors. Unlike you, we were created to help her diffuse the power and stay in control. If she's having trouble, then one of us needs to be nearby. Especially when she's sleeping, if that's when she's having the most trouble," Laran rumbled. He was taller than Julian, and almost as menacing as he glared down at Moira. My best friend didn't shrivel like a frail little flower, as most who faced the Horsemen would. She returned his glare unafraid and entirely sure of her place in my world.

"You sure this is about helping her?" Moira challenged, a feral grin gracing her lips. Rysten chuckled under his breath, and Julian threw a warning glare at Laran.

"You're not helping the situation, War," Julian said stiffly.

"The banshee doesn't understand her place," he growled back.

"*My* place? What about *your* place—"

"My place is by her side," he snapped back at her.

"Do you know how many men, demons and human, have told me that over the years?" Moira sneered. Okay then. Time to deescalate the situation before Laran tries to silence her or she blows his eardrums.

"Guys. You are both being ridiculous. The sooner you both are quiet, the sooner I get to take a shower, so shut it." Moira pursed her lips and stepped aside. Laran didn't say anything, but the tick in his jaw was telling. He was being quiet because I asked it, but the moment Moira went off again it was going to be a throw down in my bedroom.

"Originally, I thought you had longer before the transition. Now, I'm not sure. I would be more comfortable if you moved in with us in the meantime—with the banshee, if you insist," Julian added quickly as the expression on Moira's face soured.

Move in with them? Did he realize how crazy that sounded?

"You can't be serious," I said, trying to brush it off. I would have laughed at him like I did when he said I was the devil's daughter, but I'd already been proven wrong once. If that was possible, I suppose anything was. Even Julian and the Horsemen getting such a crazy idea as to want me to move in.

"I'm quite serious," Julian replied stiffly.

I could tell my reaction displeased him by the tension in his eyes, but he wasn't arguing. Not yet at least. Rysten took one look between Julian and me, perhaps sensing his brother's thinning patience now that I declined their offer. Devil knows I could feel it.

"Look, love, you don't have a living room. The insulation in the floor is ruined and it's November. In Oregon. At the moment, we won't make you do anything you don't want to, but please understand you're only putting off the inevitable," Rysten said softly. I met his jade colored eyes and softened inside. Even with his power pulsing through the room and not hidden behind a glamor, this was Rysten. The same Rysten that came to earth and learned to be more human for me. The one that tried to give me a choice, even when the other Horsemen were being ruled by their dicks and exuded nothing but pure arrogance.

"You know how crazy this sounds, right?" I asked him softly. His lips quirked up in an almost human grin, reminiscent of the boyish smile I thought he had. His real smile was more animalistic; less refined. But it was still him.

"I know, but you must understand: we're demons, Ruby. We don't think like humans do. If you were anyone else, we would take you without asking. We'd probably be halfway to Hell already. You were raised by humans, and so we're trying. For you."

Rysten was the only one of them that had mastered pretty words that could make a girl swoon, and my ability to feel the emotions of those around me told me he meant every one of them.

I bit my lip, letting the pain scatter the heat that was beginning to spread through me. The beast perked her head up and eyed Rysten thoughtfully. The words meant little to her. She was not one to be swayed by emotion. She didn't care for much outside me and mine, but in that moment, Rysten held her interest as she eyed him with something akin to want. Possession.

"*Mine*," she insisted. My lips thinned as I pushed her

aside. So not happening right now. She hissed at me, but didn't make a serious lunge for power, thankfully.

"I appreciate you giving me the choice, but I need to think on it," I said. The beast downright sulked at my non-committal answer. She could get the fuck over it. As sweet as Rysten could be, moving in with them, however temporary, was not something I needed to decide on before coffee.

I shooed them all out before anyone could try to change my mind or give the beast reason enough to surface. She was already pacing impatiently, and I knew if she came forward, they wouldn't leave without me in tow.

That knowledge alone had the possessive bitch downright gleeful that even if I didn't go now, eventually she was going to get her way.

I hoped that with coffee I could disagree with her, but there were some things that even caffeine couldn't change. The Horsemen's bond with me was one of them.

CHAPTER 3

Black particles glittered like ground up stardust as they swirled down the bathroom drain. The ash was all that remained of my living room and everything it held. I couldn't tell one spec from another, whether it was my beloved couch, the first piece of furniture I bought, or the threadbare blanket that Moira wove me when we were fifteen—I would never know. Because it was all gone.

It was only a room and they were only possessions, but they were a good portion of the only things I'd ever owned. The house itself we were still paying off, and while the money we made running Blue Ruby Ink was good...it wasn't good enough to fund these kinds of repairs amidst everything else. Not exactly like we could file a claim with insurance for starting a fire with magical blue flames while I was sleeping. I didn't need some fire investigators poking around here. No. We'd have to do this ourselves.

Worry nagged at me as I finished my shower, but there was no point. What would worrying do? Not a damn thing. I shook the heaviness that tried to descend upon me as I wrung out my hair and dried off. The towel was hardly enough to keep the bite away from the bitter cold as I opened the bathroom door. It was chillier in here than I remembered, but not cold enough for me to think much of it. I dressed quickly, donning long johns under my jeans and two thick shirts to go with my sweatshirt.

From up in his hammock, Bandit watched me curiously. I could have sworn he cocked an eyebrow at my choice of clothing.

"What? You expect me to freeze my ass off? We don't all have fur to keep us warm, you know," I said, putting my hands on my hips. He let out a chittering noise and jumped to the bed. I crossed the room in a few quiet strides, my bare feet losing feeling against the cold carpet fibers. I lifted Bandit from the bed and held him to my chest. He wasn't so keen on being cuddled like a baby right now and opted for scurrying up my front. He wrapped himself around my shoulders and neck like a poufy scarf.

"Uh uh. Not happening," Moira's voice carried from the door. I turned towards her as she crossed her arms and leaned against the frame. "Trash panda's not coming with."

I shot her a look of annoyance, burying my fingers in his fur.

"Why not? I bring him into work all the time," I said defensively.

"Because we're not going into Blue Ruby today. Fuck all, we're going to Voodoo Doughnut. He may like you a lot, but last I checked, vermin aren't allowed inside." She picked at an invisible piece of lint on her jacket. The puffy black material was sleek enough I didn't think even the plumes of ash in our living room would stick to it.

"What do you mean we're not going—"

"I took the liberty of rescheduling your Sunday appointments," she said. Her face was blank. Neutral as could be. I wasn't fooled; guilt and worry swirled inside her just below the surface. They were eating at her protective instincts, enough so that I bit off my retort about her rescheduling without asking, and simply said, "Okay."

She blinked once and cleared the surprise from her face in record time while I grabbed my boots and heavy wool socks. Bandit wasn't happy that he wasn't coming with, but in the end, a breakfast of rewarmed tilapia was enough to placate him.

The drive to Voodoo Doughnut was swift, made faster by Moira's *skilled* driving. It takes a special kind of person to put a Camry on two wheels and not bat an eyelash. Some days I wondered if she even noticed things like stop signs and traffic lights. Or maybe she did and simply thought they were mere suggestions as opposed to actual rules. Knowing her, it was entirely possible.

Pulling up outside, the parking lot was mostly empty. Only two cars and the van unloading were present. The

Pepto-Bismol pink bricks of Portland's most notorious doughnut shop were a more welcome sight than I'd realized. After eating nothing more than ice cream for over twenty-four hours, something solid would be good, even if it was more sugar. My stomach rumbled in agreement.

The shadow man from the sign above the door stared down at me as we approached the building. His eyes looked oddly real for the black abyss they were supposed to be. I frowned, but didn't comment as we walked inside, the tiled black and white floors gleaming at us in welcome. The scent of fresh doughnuts made my mouth water.

The girl at the counter smiled up at us and waved. Her hair shined white at the roots and darkened to a neon purple at the ends of her pigtails. She wore a tight t-shirt with the shop name that stopped short of her low-cut jeans, exposing her midriff and the edges of a white tattoo around her left hip bone.

"Hi there, what can I get for you ladies?" she asked. It was right about the moment we reached the counter that I noticed how pointed her teeth were. She took a breath, looking back and forth between the two of us, and her smile widened. "Apologies for the mistake," she corrected in a purr. I glanced down at the nails that were tapping against the glass counter. Wicked sharp and painted in a gleaming royal purple. "It's rare that I find two she-demons in this area. Not to mention unclaimed." Her eyes appraised us with interest.

"This isn't marked territory, is it?" Moira asked sharply, her eyes focused with an intensity that would have made a weaker demon subservient. The unknown did not lower her gaze, which made Moira's question even more pressing. For unclaimed demons to walk into another's territory, particularly a half-demon like Moira...the scenarios ranged from bad to worse.

And it was that thought alone that had the beast leaping forward.

I lunged to maintain hold, only barely beating her to it as the she-demon watched me with mercury-colored eyes. They were the most exquisite shade of silver I'd ever seen, and it threw me for a loop at identifying what kind of demon she might be.

The beast in me shifted restlessly and the unknown demon smiled.

"Relax. This area is not yet claimed. I was sent here by my master because of some...disputes going on in the area," she said with a toothy grin. It was a smile that was almost impish, but somehow darker.

"Disputes?" I asked tightly. I wasn't aware that there were clans this far north. Demons hated the cold. The imp from the Black Brothers was an outlier. At least I thought he was. Me and Moira didn't exactly stay on the up and up of the demon world here on earth. We had a hard enough time making it with the humans, so we left demons and their politics behind by the time we were seventeen. We set out to forge our own way, for a time. But it seems the demon world wasn't letting go. Not now that I had a fucking pentagram branded on my chest.

There was no hiding forever, but this was exactly why I was in no hurry to leave.

The unknown she-demon clicked her tongue, dragging it across her jagged teeth. I waited for a smear of blue blood to show, but she didn't cut herself.

"Dead demons turned up outside a night club a few days back. Or at least their ashes did. Wouldn't know anything about that, would you?" she asked slowly. I pulled my eyes from her seductively threatening tongue. I was used to drawing everything male my way, but somehow, I always felt awkward when females came looking. They were never as mindless as the men, but ever as persistent. It made me have both a certain appreciation and fair amount of wariness with all demons. After all, all it took was a brand to be claimed.

"Nope," I drawled out. "Haven't heard anything about that," I replied slowly. My heartbeat slowed to a crawl as persuasion tried to leech its way into my voice. As tempting as it was, she was bound to realize something was off if she even caught the smallest inkling of it. I was better off lying through my teeth for the time being.

The she-demon seemed to consider this, leveling me with a falsely positive stare. There was amusement hidden there, in the depths of her eyes. And something darker.

"Good to know," she said softly and clapped her hands together. The noise startled me, and I jumped back from the counter. She let out a husky laugh and started motioning to the doughnuts that were spinning around in the glass case to my left. Moira put a hand against my shoulder and made like she was trying to see around me. Her fingers dug into my skin, pumping into me her strength. Calm. I eased against her while she selected her doughnut and the unknown she-demon turned to me. Her eyes betrayed nothing. Whatever darkness was there had vanished.

"And you?" she asked. I didn't even need to think about what I was getting. I got the same thing every time.

"Triple chocolate penetration for me," I said. She smirked as she reached for the extra chocolatey doughnut. I licked my lips when a voice me made me freeze.

"Excellent choice, little succubus." Allistair's power wafted through the air. His strength was like a fog, and it pushed through every cell of my being the closer he came. It invaded my mind with dirty thoughts and constricting around my core without my permission, sharpening the need that already enslaved my body most days and nights.

I took a tight breath and turned my head only a fraction towards him. His eyes were dark, but not with need. *What the—*

I followed his stare from me to the she-demon behind the counter who was ringing up Moira. She hadn't appeared to have seen him yet, but there was no way she couldn't have heard him. The sinister little smile on her lips made me boil with contempt.

Contempt?

No, that can't be right. There's no possible—reasonable—explanation for why I may want to rip her throat out...except for the look she gave Allistair the moment

Moira turned away from the counter. Her eyes brightened with an unnatural shimmer as she waved to him.

Unable to stop myself, I let out a growl. It was soft. Silent to human ears. Yet it dripped with a rage that was completely foreign to me. The beast was pushing against my hold. She wanted to tear the demon's throat out for looking at someone that was *hers*.

"Ruby?" Moira asked. Her voice sounded far away even though she was right next to me. I couldn't answer her while the beast and I were locked in a silent battle of wills. I couldn't even look at her, because the beast demanded that we watch this other she-demon before she tried anything.

The silver-eyed demon turned her gaze from Allistair to me, and another growl escaped my lips.

"Ruby," the darkest of desires called out to me. Passion made flesh. Pure masculinity given sound. Both the beast and I were powerless to resist it. We turned as one, drawn to the voice that dared taunt us. Tempt us.

"Look at me, Ruby."

A single tantalizing finger hooked under my chin, drawing my eyes upward, only to be pulled into amber depths so vivid they looked like molten gold. The beast nearly purred as I leaned into the touch. Allistair's lips parted, breathing a taste of warmth across my face that caressed my skin.

For a moment, I was transfixed in an in-between state of reality where only Allistair and I existed. Until the door behind him opened and a group of blushing girls walked in, entirely unaware of what we were or the sticky situation they could so easily have placed them-selves in, had his presence not calmed the beast enough to retreat.

I bit my lip and turned for the door, not looking over my shoulder once at the purple-haired demon we were leaving behind.

"What happened in there, Ruby?" Moira asked, coming up on my side. The slap of the cold made me stuff my hands in my armpits while we walked. My hunger for food all but forgotten as my best friend took a hulking bite out of her doughnut. Bavarian cream drib-bled down her chin from the very aptly named Cock and Balls. The phallus shaped doughnut was her absolute favorite, and more than likely the source of the chuckle behind us.

"She started to lose control of the beast," Allistair said almost cheerfully.

"Why do you sound so excited about that?" I snapped at him. I don't even know how he found us, or why he was here, but given how the Horsemen always turned up at the most inconvenient of times, I didn't question it.

"I'm amused, little succubus," he said softly in my ear, "because she is possessive enough of me to fight you. It makes me wonder what twisted little thoughts you have hiding in that mind of yours, and all the things I can do to figure them out." I shivered and trudged forward, blaming it on the cold. He's lucky Moira didn't hear him. There would be a throw down in the parking lot.

"Keep dreaming, incubus. You forget that Moira was

there as well," I said over my shoulder. The grin fell from his lips as he considered what I said, failing to notice what I didn't say. His eyes shifting between me and my best friend as we climbed in the car.

Moira thrust the pink box at me while she maneuvered the car with one hand and annihilated her doughnut with the other. Half the cock and one of the balls were already gone and it hadn't been a minute since we'd set foot outside the store. I shook my head at her and barely contained my grin at the frown that graced Allistair's lips while he watched us pull out of the parking lot.

I shifted my eyes away from him to the sign over Voodoo Doughnut. There in the middle was the shadow man, with his gleaming black eyes. Moira turned the corner sharply and floored it onto the road. Out of the corner of my eye, just far enough that I could still see, I could have sworn the shadow man winked.

But that's not possible. It must have been a trick of the light.

ALLISTAIR

The beast was raging inside of her.

She didn't think I saw it. The way it looked out through her eyes with a challenge. She was the ultimate predator, and it made her highly possessive of anyone she deemed as hers. While the banshee may fall in that category, I was not stupid. She wants me, and her beast already thinks it owns me. It's only a matter of time until she comes around.

My would-be queen, just ripe for the taking.

But I'm getting ahead of myself here.

I needed to break through those walls and let her see that Rysten isn't the only one with a heart. However pathetic an excuse for one mine may be. I was an incubus, and the only one of us four that could understand what she was going through. At least from a sexual deprivation level.

She was brimming with power, so much so that her body was trying to find outlets, to siphon it off—and it was being made infinitely worse by how much she was starving herself.

Not that she was going to let any of us fix that in the short term.

First, I needed to find a way to patch up her mind from the damage the human caused.

Then I will devour her and show her what someone truly worthy can offer.

CHAPTER 4

We spent the afternoon cleaning ash out of every nook and cranny of our house. Well, Moira did. I was on dustpan duty and in charge of disposing it in our metal trash can out back. I probably made thirty trips outside that afternoon and ignored the shadows as they crept around my house.

The Horsemen were there, just beyond my line of sight. I couldn't see them, but I could *feel* them. Their essence called me; to more than just me. It called to the thing pacing restlessly inside. My beast didn't understand, couldn't fathom, why I bothered with cleaning the house when we could be with them. When we *should* be with them.

She couldn't understand my human emotions, when we were not human. Not even a drop. That I was raised with humans was unimportant to her. She saw my need for independence and space as cumbersome. Inconvenient. Irrational even. My desire for time to adjust was laudable in her mind, but given that I knew exactly why she pushed me and what she wanted, I wasn't inclined to listen. Not to a sociopathic entity that had very few true emotions of her own outside of desire and rage.

She goaded me. Poked. Prodded. Did anything and everything she could to try and force my hand as the sky bled from blue to black. I didn't give even an inch, because she would take a mile.

Sleep was unachievable that night. Not with my body wound so tight that I ended up staring at the ceiling for the better part of the early November morning. Bandit curled around one side of me and I could sense Moira's presence only a room away. Peace of mind never came. Just a restless and dazed drifting where time crawled at an agonizing pace. I must have blinked a thousand times because somewhere along the way, the night had passed, and morning was here.

Soft light gleamed through the cracks in my curtains, illuminating my room with the soft grey glow of the cloudy sky. Despite the outward appearance of serenity, the beast still paced within me. Not at rest, even after a night of forcing myself to stay in bed with the hopes of finding peace. Oh no, she was not the least bit put off or worn down. If anything, she was more irritable. Her frustration leaked into me and the blood in my veins sizzled with life. Right at that moment, in my sleep-deprived, pre-caffeinated haze, I realized I wasn't planning on sitting around or cleaning for another day.

I needed to get out. Do something. Otherwise the

damn beast was going to drive me crazy, or even worse, straight to the Horsemen's beds.

I jumped up and began digging through my closet, cursing under my breath at how cold it had gotten. Frigid enough that when I hunched over to dig through my pile of clean laundry, my breath frosted, turning into smoky white puffs in front of me. My lips thinned as I pulled on a pair of jeans over the long johns I wore to bed. The rips in the front of them showed the dark grey material beneath, giving me at least some kind of protection from the chill. I pulled on a t-shirt and two sweatshirts to finish myself off. It was going to be cold as balls outside, but I wanted short sleeves if I was going into Blue Ruby today. I never liked to tattoo in long sleeves. They felt constricting. Tight. Particularly in some of the awkward positions I have to get into to work.

Just as I finished lacing up my boots, Moira appeared in the doorway of my room, steaming cup of coffee in hand.

"Going somewhere?" she asked. Her tone was testing, not quite bossy, but the displeasure was there. She crossed her skinny green arms over her chest and cocked her head.

"Yep. I have four clients today, two of which I had to reschedule with last week. Not to mention whoever else rescheduled yesterday," I replied, equally as terse. From his hammock in the corner, Bandit flung himself at me, wrapping his arms around my neck. He let out the most pathetic mewling noises ever, and I'm pretty sure they were all for effect.

"Are you sure? Even the trash panda is worried about you. Maybe it's better you stay home for another day," she said as Bandit let out another screech in my ear. His tiny paws grabbed at me as his claws dug into the back of my neck.

"I've already stayed home for two days. I broke my tradition of going to Martha's every Saturday, and I have never missed one in ten years. I'm not staying locked in the house anymore. You and Bandit can get over it. We still have bills to pay and a tattoo parlor to run," I said resolutely. The raccoon hanging around my neck literally started quivering and bawled like a fucking baby.

For fuck's sake.

A knock, or pounding rather, interrupted us. Bandit shut his trap and climbed on my shoulder, switching modes from whining little shit to vigilante protector. I shook my head and muttered,

"Unbelievable…"

Moira followed behind me as I approached the front door. I put my hand to the lock as I stared through the little peephole. Never in my life had I bothered to check before opening the door. Until now. I guess being drugged, molested, and then almost kidnapped would do that to you.

"Ruby, I know you're there, love. Why don't you open the door for me?" Rysten called. His dark green eyes stared at the hole in the door. His sandy blonde curls, Miami Beach t-shirt, and trendy jacket were so misleading for what lurked beneath his glamor. His dark powers weren't what made me lock the doors, as formidable as they were.

Silently, I cracked it open.

"There you are. I've been worried. Allistair told us you had a little problem yesterday with keeping the beast at bay. I thought I might come spend the day with you," he said gently. His hand was more insistent than his words as he pushed the door open further. Just wide enough to see Bandit bolstered to my shoulder, and Moira standing next to me with her arms crossed over her chest. "That one"—he motioned to Moira and his jaw ticked—"sent me away last night when I tried to check in on you."

"Me?" Moira gasped innocently, looking from side to side before placing a hand to her chest. She opened her mouth in pretend shock. Rysten threw a glare in her direction and she dropped the façade, cackling even though she was only doing what I asked her. But who was I to ruin her fun?

"Well, as you can see, I'm taken care of and I'm actually running a bit late for work..." My voice trailed off as the other three Horsemen stepped into view from the side of the house, where I could only assume they were hiding.

"I can take you to work," he said. His voice was falsely cheerful. Hopeful.

"Or we all can," Laran cut in, placing his hand on Rysten's shoulder in such a way that would have been supportive, even brotherly, if he weren't squeezing the crap out of him. Yeah, subtlety wasn't War's strong suit.

"There's not enough room," I said. Laran had the audacity to cut his eyes towards my VW bug and actually consider it. Even when a frown graced his lips, he didn't yield.

"We could—"

I held up a hand to stop him. To both my surprise and pleasure, he stopped talking. The beast purred.

"I know you guys mean well, but I need you to give me time to think about things. Okay?" I asked. Next to me, Moira muttered, "Some space wouldn't hurt either."

Both men cut her harsh looks and I let out an exasperated sigh. My nerves were just too frayed to put up with the bickering today. Sleep deprivation wasn't treating me kind and the snarling beast inside me was royally pissed.

"Can I have a minute, Moira?" She gave me a cool look that promised this wasn't over as she strode away, her bathrobe stirring in the breeze.

The four watched me reproachfully, their faces unreadable, but all emotions splayed open for me to see. It was a spectrum that ranged from an ever-present controlled rage, to the throbbing intensity of desire that invaded every cell of my body, making the hairs on my arms stand on end.

"Look guys, I'm heading into work. Without you. Any of you. I need the day to just try to pretend that everything is okay. That it's *normal*. Do you understand?" I asked slowly. A flash of pain shone in Rysten's eyes, but he smiled nonetheless.

"Of course, love. If that's what you need," he replied.

Laran opened his mouth to disagree and Allistair grasped his shoulder.

"Let's go for a walk, War," Allistair said briskly. His golden eyes flashed to mine, and then they were gone, leaving only Rysten and Julian on my doorstep. The resemblance between them was striking, but it was only skin deep. When you really looked at them, there couldn't be two people more different.

Rysten was kind, easy to laugh and quick to smile. He was the hottie-next-door you always dreamed about. The guy that has his pick of girls but marries his high school sweetheart and settles for life. The kind that every girl wants to date, and every guy is friends with, and across it all, you just can't help but love him. He's the sweet guy. The good guy...but Julian was entirely different.

He didn't strike me as the type of bad boy that roamed from woman to woman. He was more reserved than that. More guarded. There was this air to him that had an edge of something stronger, harder than steel. Colder than ice. Darker than even death. Julian wasn't a bad boy or the boy next door. He was the kind that lived in the darkness. That fostered it. Nurtured it. The kind of man that mothers warn their daughters about. The kind that no matter how smart a girl you are, no woman could possibly say no to.

He was the kind that may not leave a string of hearts in his wake, but when he did find someone...

Heaven and Hell will not be able to separate them. Not even God herself.

My cheeks warmed and I silently cursed my pasty cheeks.

"Ruby?" The question brought my comparing them to a grinding halt. I drew my eyes away from Julian's lips, the lips I had been staring at so intently and not realized it.

"Yes?" I asked, slightly breathless.

"Everything alright, love?" Rysten asked slowly. Their eyes were focused on me with an intensity both sinfully delicious and unnerving at the same time. Lucky for me, I was pretty sure my thoughts were my own. Unlike me, I didn't think they could read emotions. Except maybe Allistair...

"Yep," I drawled out. "I'm just tired and still processing everything. Let me have today to get back in the swing of things..." I trailed off at the look the brothers were sharing. It was unreadable, but undeniably there. "Is there something you have to say?" I snapped. The up and downs between me and the beast were giving me whiplash. One moment I was turned on and the next I was agitated. Maybe it was me coping. Maybe it was the transition. But it was probably just the Horsemen.

Rysten approached me. Unlike Laran, who had no issue crowding my space, or Allistair, who wore a wicked sneer as he tempted me, Rysten simply stopped short and took my hand in his. Bandit grumbled under his breath but settled back on my shoulder, the closest that he ever comes to accepting anyone outside of me and Moira.

"I can only imagine how hard this is right now."

Rysten's words sounded tight with an unnamable emotion that I didn't want to feel. I wondered if it was his inability to truly empathize, or sympathy at the situation their arrival had put me in. "But you need to have a guard around you at all times now, love. We can wait to talk about the changes coming, but please don't ask us to leave. We can't. Not when one of the demons who attacked you still roams free."

I sighed deeply, running my free hand over my face. I didn't like it. I didn't like any of this. I planned to keep pushing back until there was no other choice, but maybe for today having one of them with me wouldn't be the worst thing in the world. The beast was restless and called for blood, and I didn't want to give her a chance to spill it. As much as I hated to admit it, they soothed her.

Keeping her calm was just as important as keeping bloodthirsty imps away. My control over her, even if it was barely, was the only reason they were still giving me choices and letting me decide things for myself.

"Fine, *one of you* can come with me today, but this doesn't mean I'm moving in or agreeing to being watched twenty-four-seven. It just means I don't feel like arguing today. Got it?" Rysten nodded, a smirk playing on the corners of his lips. Beside him, Julian's expression turned cold, his emotions laced with something almost like...jealousy?

I raised my eyes to his, the question almost playing on my lips. I didn't feel it was my place to ask, but before I could decide, he turned sharply and strode towards the shade of a large conifer.

"Keep an eye on her. One of the other's will switch in this afternoon, if she'll let us." His voice was icy. Curt. The long-sleeve shirt he wore bunched around his shoulders where the muscles contracted, taut with tension. He didn't spare a glance over his shoulder as he strode into the shadows and disappeared like he was never here at all.

RYSTEN

He had no reason to be pissed at me.

He knew exactly how this was going to go down the moment all four of us laid eyes on her. She's not just an infatuation, and she never will be. He was daft for continuing to hold her at arm's length while expecting the rest of us to do so as well.

We weren't just her guardians anymore, even though she herself did not want to see it.

Her beast chose us.

I knew the moment I saw her standing at the door, crossing her arms over her chest like she could cover the truth. She's formed an attachment, to each of us, and the beast accepted it.

Not that it would have ever accepted anyone else. Humans were not even worth that predator's attention and other male-demons would not be able to handle it, or her.

She was more her father's daughter than she realized, and Lola would have been proud.

I've never met a she-demon that I felt truly possessive over. It's difficult when you know that the one you were created for may come along at any point, but never in my wildest dreams did I imagine that very she-demon would be the one to draw out the darkness.

To goad it. Rile it up.

And make me want to slaughter any male outside of us who dared get close to her.

CHAPTER 5

The bell jingled on the front door of Blue Ruby Ink.

"We're closed for lunch right now," I said without looking up. Rysten and Moira had left only minutes ago to find lunch for us while I completed the revisions to the design a client requested.

"We need to have a little chat, you an' I."

The thick southern drawl was unmistakable.

As was the blonde haired, blue-eyed beauty behind it.

"What do you want, Kendall?" My words were terse; laced with a hint of the beast I could not hide. I was going to need to make this little meeting short, or risk her upsetting the dark entity that disliked everything she represented.

"Josh is missin'," she started, her voice quivering a fraction as she said it.

I set the pencil down and slid the design aside, placing it in a seal-tight envelope to protect it from

Moira's klutziness and any *accidental* spills that Kendall was prone to.

"I'm not certain why you're coming to me with this. We broke up over six weeks ago," I said lightly. Her glistening eyes hardened at my dismissive tone, but not for one second did I believe she was here for anything good.

"I *know* he was still seein' you, Ruby. And now he's up an' disappeared. I haven't heard from him since Friday..." She swallowed hard, fighting her wasted tears. Part of me wanted to tell her to keep her tears; save them for someone worthy. Someone who wouldn't be with her while still pining for his ex like a dog in heat. The rest of me knew not to believe any show she put on.

"Well, I haven't seen him. So I don't know what to—"

"Don't lie to me!" she snapped. I blinked in surprise but didn't react otherwise as Kendall smoothed her bubblegum pink dress. "I'm givin' you the chance to confess your sins an' tell me where he is." Angry tears burst through causing her black mascara to streak down her cheeks. She didn't outright cry or sob, but the venom that filled her eyes was telling.

"I don't know what you're talking about."

I didn't even miss a beat in my response because I'd planned for this moment since I woke up from that nightmare at Pandora's Box. Kendall was nearly as obsessive as he was, and I knew that as much as the Horsemen assured me it would be like he never existed, this wouldn't go away.

Sure, they could cover up his death, but they couldn't

cover up his life. He wasn't a demon. He was human. A weak-willed human that lost his mind from a desire I caused but didn't know how to undo.

I couldn't bring myself to feel bad, not when his very name awoke memories of that night. Nightmares of lying on a conference table, drugged out of my mind and unable to move while he dry humped my body and molested me.

He would have raped me if the Horsemen hadn't shown, and so I would not feel guilty.

Not for him.

Kendall dabbed at her eyes and cheeks with a handkerchief, erasing the evidence of tears. A cruel smile stole her lips as she reached inside her purse and withdrew a single sheet of paper.

She crossed the space between us and extended her hand.

Devil save me.

It was a photo. Of Josh and me. At the bar in Pandora's Box.

This couldn't have been taken more than an hour before he tried to rape me.

Before he groped me, and undressed me, and—I was going to be sick.

Blood roared in my veins as I toppled sideways from the chair. The onslaught to my system hit me fast and sudden as I tried to heave up food that wasn't there. My stomach rolled as the world went sideways and my connection to the outside severed.

I'd never had a panic attack in my life, despite all the bad things that had happened.

I took those memories, even as they were happening, and stored them in a box. Placed inside a vault where I would lock it away, never to see the light of day again.

That was how it worked. How I coped.

I didn't have panic or anxiety. I lived my life, accepting that it happened but forgetting a little more every day.

Until I couldn't.

"What in the name of—" Kendall started screaming. I went from hearing nothing, being trapped in a bubble of my own creation, to being yanked back into a reality where the picture in her hand made me sick to my stomach.

He's dead. He can no longer harm you.

I swallowed hard, taking in deep breaths as the door to the shop slammed open.

I didn't have to look to know that Moira and Rysten had returned. Their combined emotions were like jumper cables to my heart. The fear receded as the cold fury of an entity that very much wanted to burn her alive took its place.

I was still in control, but hanging on by a thread.

"Kendall, I don't know what the fuck you are doing here, but if you don't walk out right now, you're leaving in a body bag. You hear me?" Moira didn't scream. She didn't shout. Hell, she didn't even raise her voice. She let the calm chill of her words settle over us and wrap around Kendall, using the quiet to speak her intentions louder than the words themselves.

"Th-thi-this isn't over! I know what happened! I know the *truth!*" she screamed and then she was gone.

The truth? She didn't know that. I doubt any of them knew the whole truth as to what happened that night. I knew the truth, because I'd seen it before.

Josh's case was not specific to him. It was the same story for most males that crossed my path. I'd accepted that and learned to live with it a long time ago. Or so I thought.

Moira hugged me and whispered promises of revenge. She meant to soothe me. To calm me.

Right there in the place I chose to leave my mark on this world, I decided that this would not break me. Kendall said this wasn't over, and I would be ready when she returned. Ready to let the lies run from my lips.

Even if I cared nothing for Josh, it was not the truth that mattered here. Only what Kendall saw as the truth, and for all his affections and obsessive thoughts—I was still the one, even in death, paying the price.

CHAPTER 6

Moira and I didn't speak on it as the day went on, but I could sense her worried glances. Both what she directed at me as well as the ones shared with Rysten. I locked myself in my office after my last client left and didn't come out, even when she knocked and told me she was leaving. I didn't feel like seeing anyone.

Alone with nothing but my own thoughts, I chewed at the corner of my thumbnail and flipped through my files for designs to work on. It wasn't much, but it was something.

The first design I completed was done in pencil. A simple black and white drawing of a rose for a mother who lost her daughter as a baby. The second was a tempest, quite literally, done in the most brilliant of blues and yellows. The sky was clad with lightning and the clouds rolled so effortlessly they could have been real. This one was for an older woman who had once been a sailor. She told me of the skies and the sea, and how they tried to claim her life again and again. She endured, much like the mother had when her daughter died. That old woman had cancer now, but she wanted a sleeve on her right arm as a reminder of what she's been through. An aid, to weather the storm.

It was beautiful. One of my best pieces, and I hadn't even shown her yet. I smiled, running the tip of my finger around the heavy Aegean clouds dusted with traces of lapis blue. The words replayed over and over in my mind: *an aid to weather the storm.*

People had faced far worse things than I and lived to smile again. To fight again. Hell, I usually was not one to be thrown so far off track from myself that a picture could blindside me like it had. So what had changed?

Was it me? Was it the Horsemen? I know I didn't care for Josh enough that it was his actions that stirred me. I'd been down that path before, with devils and demons that were stronger than him. Was that it? That he was weak, and yet he'd bested me? But could you even call that besting when he had to drug me to do it?

My mind was a place of colors and secrets, of paradigms and lies. I did not hurt easily, but little things made me snap. I didn't consider myself a liar, but my entire existence was one fat fucking lie. I was created to be a ruler, and not just any ruler. The ruler of Hell.

Queen of the Underworld.

But a fucking picture brought me to my knees. There was something so right about that, and yet so cruel. After all, I wasn't the one who died that night. I'm just the one that has to live with everyone else's mistakes. The one that got drugged, not once, but twice—thanks to the imp that Laran pissed off for touching me. Of course, he wouldn't have been touching me if we hadn't gone there in the first place. Could I actually blame him for taking me there? No. Not as much as I could blame Josh for his actions. I didn't regret his death, and I still don't. But that doesn't mean I'm unaffected either.

Seeing that, doing that, it fucks with your head, and this wasn't the first time it's happened. It's just the first time it's happened with the Horsemen. What about next time? What happens when we go to Hell? I'd woefully turned a blind eye to the demon world because I didn't want to see it, but now it's here and it can't be denied.

Fuck it all.

I jumped up from my desk and stored the artwork away where it couldn't be ruined from spilt coffee or takeout tacos. I grabbed my purse and washed my hands, cleaning away the remaining residue from the colored pencils. The water bled blue and yellow, turning a sickly shade of green. I wasn't one to believe in omens. That was a different kind of demon, but the color didn't sit well with me.

The shop was quiet when I locked up and the sun was long asleep. An obsidian sky stared back at me as I stepped out from the light of Blue Ruby Ink.

Calm brushed against my skin and the beast settled for the first time today. It was not a natural calm; not something I gave myself, but a gift from another.

"I take it that it's your turn?" I asked softly. Allistair stepped out of the shadows. The sharpness of his high cheekbones was particularly prominent tonight against his alabaster skin. During the day, he was devastatingly handsome, but at night...he was somehow more. The light in his eyes shined brighter, and the lushness of his dark curls just begged to be touched. At night, Allistair was the most beautiful creature I'd ever seen.

The corners of his mouth turned up into a knowing smile.

"Let's go for a ride," he replied. On most nights, I probably would have protested, given where I ended up last time I let a Horseman take me somewhere without telling me.

But Allistair wasn't Laran, and I was a different kind of Ruby now.

He extended his hand, and all I could think about was an *aid to weather the storm*. I didn't know who I was right now. I was Ruby. I was Lucifer's Daughter. I was a monster. I was...living the best I could in our messed-up world and doing the best I can.

But sometimes, you just gotta let a devil take the wheel.

I DIDN'T ASK him where we were going as the lights streaked by like shooting stars. Allistair had the nicest car I'd ever ridden in. Black leather, heated seats, and a cup of tea waiting in the cup holder. I wrapped my hands around the steaming cup, trying to leech its warmth away as I took a small sip.

Earl Grey with a hint of honey and a splash of milk. Perfect.

I let out a small sigh. This calm was fabricated from him. Instinctually, I knew that.

In reality, I didn't care where we went as long as it didn't end.

"How's the tea?" he asked.

Small talk. It was such a very human thing to do. I didn't know whether I should be thankful or annoyed that he was bothering at all.

"It's perfect," I replied without turning his way. It was easier not to focus on anything. The lights were brilliant and beautiful, carrying with them all my melancholy as they passed by.

"Excellent," he said. I smiled, just the briefest lift of my lips at the pride in his voice. I'd been wondering if Rysten told him how I liked my tea as a way to cheer me, but maybe Allistair paid attention more than I realized.

The car descended into silence for another moment. This one longer than the first, so long in fact, that the lights were becoming fewer and fewer. We were leaving the city.

The thought both had me intrigued and mildly nervous, but I kept quiet because if he were smuggling me away somewhere for any length of time, I knew the other three would be here, too.

"You know," Allistair said, breaking the silence, "I know what you're going through. Right now." I tensed, and his hand slipped from the steering wheel as he reached across and took my hand from my lap. "You don't have to say anything. I don't expect you to. I'd just like you to listen."

And I did. The blood in my veins heated at his very touch. It wasn't a sexual touch, nor was it fraught with his own messy emotions. Instead it was... kind. Reassuring. He wasn't holding my hand like a possessive prick, but instead to offer the only kind of comfort that I was always deprived of.

And then he said the last thing I ever expected him to say.

"In all my time, both in this world and ours, I have only ever fallen in love once." Even in the dark cab of the car I could sense his eyes watching me. "As someone raised among humans, you might find it surprising that it only ever happened once," he continued. "But as a woman who is half-succubus, I think you can understand.

"I have lived for thousands and thousands of years, watching women do anything in the name of what they call love. I have seen women kill themselves, their lovers, even other women they thought were a threat...just to get to me.

"In the beginning, I struggled with the blame and where it lay when I realized there was little I could do to stop them. Eventually the guilt faded, replaced by anger at the women for being so stupid. For not seeing what I thought was obvious. For not seeing the *love* wasn't real —or so I thought at the time." That almost pulled a scoff from my lips, had I not been so speechless at his confession. He was Famine, one of the Four Horsemen...and still just a male at heart. Except unlike the men of earth, demons were not confined by gender roles and stereotypes. We saw ourselves as we were and did not apologize for it. In some ways that made us, him, better than the people of earth.

I kept my thoughts to myself as he continued.

"And then eventually I did fall in love with someone. A female that was forbidden in every way, but I could not stop myself. I was as caught up in it as the foolish women who'd chased me for centuries. Until I wasn't."

"What?" The question popped from my lips before I could stop myself. Allistair smiled, but there was nothing kind about it. If his hand weren't wrapped around mine, I would be scared shitless at the hateful smile he wore.

"The falling out is unimportant. The moral of the story was that the female and I split up, and we went our separate ways. She is the only one I have ever been able to do that with and it not end in bloodshed. Do you know why that is?"

I shook my head and the car came rolling to a stop. I didn't recognize where we were, only that the headlights stared off into an abyss where only the night sky reigned.

"Because they were beneath me. I was created to be strong enough to rival you, to ground you when it was needed. Women, she-demons, they were not strong enough to combat that. They were beneath me. Just because we wear the same form does not change that. I cannot apologize for being what I was created to be, any more than a hellhound can apologize for being loyal."

I was starting to see exactly where he was going, and

as someone raised among humans... I didn't know where I fell with it.

"I can't be some mindless person that just walks around killing people. That's not me, that's—" I stopped myself short from admitting those dark desires aloud.

"The beast?" he asked softly.

I bit my lip, nodding my reply.

"You were created to be the ultimate predator. The one that can keep our kind in line." He said it so simply; like that's all there was to it.

"And what if I don't want to be?" I asked.

"Don't want to be the beast, or don't want to be a succubus?" he countered, another smile playing on his lips.

"Both." He actually had the nerve to laugh.

"I don't think it's that you don't want to be them. I think it's your misconceptions of who you are and who you think you need to be. I think you're apologizing for existing, because you think that without you, things would have been different for all the men that crossed your path."

Devil save me. He was either brilliant, or a much better manipulator than I gave him credit for. I was pretty sure I was fucked either way.

"And what would you have me do?"

"Stop apologizing. Be who you are and be unashamed. I know that you want to. I can see it in your eyes. This world has done nothing for you, and yet you bleed for it. Why? You don't feel bad for the pig when you eat the bacon. Why do you feel bad for the man that hurt you?"

I shook my head. "It's not Josh I feel bad for." His hand tightened around mine briefly before he pulled away.

"Come with me."

We opened our doors and welcomed the night as an icy breeze ran over me. My ponytail whipped away from my face, a slave to the current that caught it. I walked around the front of the car, taking in deep breaths of air. It tasted different out here. Cleaner. Crisper. My boots crunched on the frosted grass as I followed the head-lights to the edge of the ravine.

I gasped as I looked down. At that same moment, the lights clicked off.

Darkness sprang from the shadows, bathing me in night. I didn't move an inch as I took in the view from hundreds of feet above. I couldn't make out the surface below us, where the rock face ended, and the dark lake began. I wouldn't have known it was water at all, if not for the two moons. One up in the sky and the other down below it, settled on the horizon. The ripples in the water scattered the light of the stars, fragmenting the vision of space around us.

"I've never seen anything quite like it," I whispered.

In a void where sound is violent, a whisper became a shout.

"I thought you might like it. Our kind have a longing for beautiful things," he murmured. Strong fingers settled against my lower back, and even through three layers of clothing, my skin flamed. "We also seek out thrills and out of this world experiences," he continued.

The heat was joined by a prickling sensation. A warning?

"Do you trust me?" he asked, his lips grazed my ear and there was nothing friendly about this touch.

My breath stalled in my throat as my mouth hung open. Allistair moved behind me as he nipped my earlobe, the heat of his breathe tingling against my skin. I came alive in the flip of a switch, instantly feeling the aching throb between my legs.

"Do you trust me?" he repeated.

Did I trust him? Here? Now? That was a hefty request. His fingers fisted in the fabric of my sweatshirt, bunching it around my back.

If I was going to make bad choices, I may as well enjoy them.

"Yes," I whispered.

"Keep your eyes open," he replied.

And then he pushed me.

CHAPTER 7

I fell through the stars waiting for the moment I would hit the water and die.

It's a strange thing being this close to death. Oddly freeing in a sense, as the inevitable washed over me. I probably had no more than a hundred feet left to drop, and while I could be asking myself all sorts of questions like, "How could he do this?" or "Why me?" The only thing I actually found myself hoping for was that Moira and Bandit would take care of each other.

The water rose up faster and the freeing feeling in my chest constricted. Wasn't there a saying that death was easy and life was hard? I was going to find out. Lucifer's daughter or not, I doubted a fall from several hundred feet was survivable.

Well, this is it. Your famous last words were trusting the guy that pushed you.

I hope Moira gives him hell.

My own reflection rose up to greet me, and I waited for the impact.

And waited.

And—

My body slammed into someone else. The impact rattled my bones, but their strength held me firm, an arm cradled under my leg and another cradled against my back. I hadn't died. I blinked and my head swiveled around. The midnight sky was the same, but there was a ridge just like the one I'd been pushed from...I frowned and swung my head back to see if the car was where I remembered it. This was just too weird. My vision was blocked by whoever's body I clung to. I followed the rise and fall of his chest up to the curve of his neck and stark cheekbones. All the way to the amber eyes that stared back.

All thoughts of dying aside, my fury clawed its way forward to greet him.

"You motherfucking bastard! How dare you push me off a—"

"You're not dead, are you?" he asked.

"No! But that's not the—"

"And you're not hurt at all, right?"

"Well no, but I'm pissed you even thought—"

"Then what are you mad about?" I could almost believe he was genuinely unaware that this was fucked up. Almost. If he hadn't been smirking down at me. He was every bit the prick I thought he was.

"Fuck you," I spat.

Allistair let out a dark chuckle. "Is that an open invitation?"

I let out an inhuman growl and bunched up my fists.

"Put me down," I snapped. Allistair swung me onto my feet but kept his arm around me. I pushed at him and tried to step away, but my legs failed me. The world tilted on its axis as vertigo hit me. "Wow," I croaked. The second my vision cleared, and my legs were my own again, I turned on Allistair. He grinned down at me, not manically, but still clearly out of his mind.

I took a swing at his face.

"Ow, man! What the fuck are you made of?" I swore angrily, shaking my hand out. Fingers dug into my right hip, holding me in place. If he were human, he'd be bruised and on the floor, just like the punk that tried to rob me. But Allistair wasn't human. Hell, he wasn't even a demon, really. He was something more.

"Did you just punch me?" he asked, working his jaw out.

"Did you just push me off a fucking cliff?" I replied. His clutch on my hip tightened and I lay my hand over his, gliding up his forearm and scraping my nails down.

Before he pushed me, before the out-of-body experience, before I thought I was about to die, I had been aroused. His presence was enough, but his touch ignited something in me every time. Then when, I didn't die, I was pissed. I wanted to hurt him. Now I just wanted him. Somehow it seems we've come full circle. My emotions swirled together in a dangerous and promising tempest within me, just waiting to be unleashed.

"Just when I think I have you figured out, you go and surprise me again," he murmured, letting his other hand drop from his face and resting it on the other side of my hip. My mouth went dry as all the insults and curses in the world left me. "It's rather refreshing, you know," he continued, leaning back to sit on the hood of his car. His hands were slowly drawing me closer. I stepped into the space between his legs and pressed my icy hands onto the curvature of his chest. In the pale moonlight, his eyes darkened from amber to bronze, drawing me in deeper.

My inner beast purred. She liked this exchange. And she wanted more.

Never breaking eye contact, I leaned into him, running my tongue over my lips, my intentions clear. The hands at my waist slipped beneath the thick material of my many layers. Hot but cold, his fingers brushed the outline of my hip bones, along the edge of my pants.

Feeling almost out of control, my body jerked towards him knowing he could give me more of what I craved so deeply. I could never before be with a man in this capacity. The world of possibility left me wanting, and more than a little needy.

"So responsive," he said huskily. His breath fanned my face as a sigh escaped my lips; his hand splayed across my back, beneath my shirt, moving to pull me in and close the space between us. I slid my hands up over his shoulders to rest at the base of his neck. My fingers brushed against stray curls of obsidian hair and tightened around the soft locks.

Allistair let out a low groan and captured my mouth with his.

His lips were not hesitant or sweet as they sought out mine and devoured me wholly. Allistair was not the kind of man to be gentle in his endeavors. Like me, there was something inside him that fed on the need and sexuality in weaker beings, and it was a downright high to taste something equal. One of his hands shifted from the grip on my back to the fabric of my bra. His dexterous fingers, skilled in seeking what they wanted, squeezed sharply, freeing my breasts.

My mouth opened more as I moaned into his mouth and he kissed me deeper, his tongue searching. He tasted of want, rich scotch, and something entirely his own. I clung to him, meeting his controlled ravaging with a fierceness that I could not contain. My fingers fisted in his hair, pulling hard, and the breath hissed between his lips, his mouth breaking from mine.

"Be careful, little succubus. My control only goes so far. I've yet to feed since I met you," he whispered against my skin. His warning had the opposite effect, only increasing my desire for him. I leaned forward, taking his bottom lip in my mouth and scraping it lightly with my teeth, sucking while I pulled away slowly.

He reached beneath the loose bra cup, palming my breast, grazing the taut peak and teasing me. Cool fingers grasped my nipple, tugging it just enough to bring me to the edge of pleasure and pain. The sensation shot straight between my legs as an ache began to build. I bit his lip as payment.

He cursed sharply and drew away. His tongue flicked out, tasting his blood on his lips. I stared at him, cocking my eyebrow, daring him to respond.

"You're savage in your desires," he said. I couldn't read his tone, but there was a wickedness to his smile. Surprise, challenge, amusement: he was making a mental note for what he would have in store for me later. His eyes didn't leave mine as he reached down and clamped his hand over the apex between my thighs. I rocked my hips into him while he watched me with dark and hungry eyes.

Right here, right now, I wasn't Ruby, and I wasn't the beast. I was a sexual being consumed by a burning need that ached within me every single day, never sated, apart from the weak relief I could find with my own hand beneath the covers late at night.

I relished the pressure of his palm over my jeans, using three fingers to rub me back and forth along the seam, the fabric blocking contact but allowing the sensation to build me up. I matched his rhythm, rubbing myself against him. Allistair would give, but I had to play by *his* rules. That was my job in this game. To take what I was given. To do as I was told. But I couldn't help myself. I ground harder against his hand, wanting more.

His hand stopped and a growl started in my chest.

"Careful. I didn't bring you out here to fuck you, but I won't leave you like this so close to transition," he groaned. I gave his hair a sharp tug and he pinned me with a glare. "You have to behave if you want it. I'm hard and fucking starving. For me to feed without fucking, I need concentration. Something I won't have if you continue biting and pulling my hair. Can you be good?" His words held the promise of what I wanted most right now. I loosened my grip on him and nodded.

He gave me a dark smile as the hand on my breast tightened again and I breathed a low moan in pleasure and relief. I'd been here before. I knew what he wanted, and I wanted to give it. The look he rewarded me with almost had me climaxing on the spot.

Allistair pulled his hand from between my thighs and made a turning motion in the air, silently telling me to turn around . I froze and cocked an eyebrow, but I did as I was told, ignoring the smirk on his lips just before he disappeared from view. I was faced with the night sky as he pulled my body back against his.

With one hand he brushed my hair to the side, while his lips grazed my skin and bit into the pulse on my neck. My breath hitched in my throat, but I didn't move. I didn't dare grind my ass onto his rock-hard cock that was flush against it.

"Mmmm, I like you this way," he murmured. I opened my mouth to reply, but one of his hands slipped underneath my shirt and flicked open the button on my jeans. My heart ricocheted in my chest.

He slowly unzipped the fly on my pants, taking his merry time. The only thing that made it bearable were the faint kisses he was leaving along my neck. His cool lips on my burning skin was a trail of straight ecstasy. He nibbled as he went, alternating sharp bites and sucking at patches of my bare flesh. I would never be this patient or play this game with anyone else. With Allistair it came naturally. I *wanted* to do as I was told; to please him. I wanted him to please me.

He tugged my jeans down a few inches and my excitement spiked. His fingers slipped inside my jeans and rubbed my clit through my panties. I couldn't help it when my body jerked in response, my ass pushing against his cock. He nipped my neck in warning and I quickly regained control. My head lolled to the side, begging for more.

"Good girl," he praised. I moaned as he pushed my panties aside, his skillful fingers entering my slick folds. I cried into the night as I tried to keep still, to play our game, my leg twitching with anticipation, my body screaming for him to make me come. Allistair hummed his approval against my neck as he massaged his fingers in deeper. The palm of his hand resting over my clit, rubbing me while he brought me closer.

"Please!" It was a guttural, useless cry. He wouldn't give me my release until he was good and ready.

"Where are my fingers? I want to hear you say it."

What...?

Through clenched teeth, I growled at him in frustration. "No..."

"I want you to tell me. I want you to say it."

Focusing on the pleasure, clenching my jaw, I was determined not to say the words.

He slowed his hand and desperation flooded me. "Where are my fingers, Ruby?" he repeated firmly, pushing in deeper as he pressed against my g-spot, sending a shock through my limbs as he sped up inside me.

"Your fingers...are in...my pussy," I managed to breathe out as my climax built further, not wanting him to stop.

"And what do you want?"

"I want you to make me come. Please make me come. Please..."

"Hmmm," he murmured. "I like the way you beg. Maybe another night we can see how many sweet sounds I can draw from those lips. I still plan on making you scream."

I kept as still as I could while the ache pulled at me, his pressure deepened, and his rhythm increased. I could feel my entire body twitching on the brink of release.

For some women, his controlling nature would have been a turn off. Hell, I didn't understand why it did the things it did to me. Usually I wanted to throttle him, but for some reason, my anger was lost when his fingers were buried inside me and I did and said things I didn't understand.

"Say my name when you come," he demanded.

I didn't have the power to tell him he was a bastard as my orgasm hit me. My head tilted back as I clenched around his fingers and I gave up being good for the reckless abandon of riding it out. "Allistair!" I choked. My hands wrapped around his thighs on either side of me, clawing at the material of his slacks, pressing myself closer to him. Feeling him against me, riding and grinding in time as his fingers continued to sweep inside me. A wave of euphoria pounded though my muscles, still spasming around his fingers. Amongst it all, there was this faint twinge inside of me as something fanned the flames and made my pleasure last longer than ever before.

Is he feeding? I wasn't sure. I'd never been with an incubus, so I didn't know what to expect, but the intense heat that flooded me was more than welcome.

I wanted more.

I pressed back against his hard length, sliding my ass up and down, reaching around for the buckle on Allistair's slacks. His sharp intake of breath made the beast purr. I pulled at his belt, but he froze instantly. He pulled away from me and pushed me out of the confines of his arms.

"I—" I swallowed the statement in my throat. I turned to look at him, speechless at his sudden and icy rejection. I fumbled as I tugged my jeans back up and hastily buttoned them.

"It's okay. You caught me off guard. I've never had— never mind. The point is it's not happening tonight." Allistair didn't normally have jarred speech, but maybe I was having more of an effect on him than I'd realized. He pulled away from the car in a fluid motion and approached me gingerly. This hot and cold attitude was getting on my last nerve. What was it he said about apologizing for things?

Oh, yeah. *Don't.*

If he wanted to be a dick, then I was just fine getting off while he got none. I crossed my arms over my chest as he raised a hand to my face and brushed his thumb over my lips. To my credit, I didn't lean into him for once.

"I didn't mean to—"

"Save it. You're still not forgiven for pushing me off a cliff." With my head clear and my body relaxed, I pushed his hand away and strode back to the car. We didn't speak as we both got in and he started the engine. The dashboard lit up, reflecting the time. It was a little past two in the morning, and I was devil knows where with him. I scowled at the expanse before us as he pulled away.

"So why did you bring me out here, huh?" I asked as he pulled onto the interstate.

"I wanted to show you where I go to relax when my burdens get too heavy from time to time. I thought you would appreciate it." His knuckles tightened against the steering wheel, but he kept his voice level when he spoke.

"You pushed me off a fucking cliff. I thought I was going to die—"

"And how did that feel?"

"I—I don't know," I stammered. "That's not the fucking point!"

"That's exactly the point," he replied. I eyed him cautiously. This was some kind of game, I could feel it. He was fucking with my mind, but I'd yet to see how.

"You wanted me to think I would die?" I asked in a shaky breath.

"I wanted you to find yourself, even if only for a moment. The cliff I pushed you off is where an entrance to Hell used to be. It was closed centuries ago. With the portal no longer active, it acts like a feedback loop. You can jump as many times as you like, and it will always spit you back out. I took you there because it's where I go when I'm faced with tough choices. It's an instinctual response to thinking you are going to die. You realize what matters, and it's the most freeing thing I have ever felt in my existence."

Freeing. Isn't that the word I used while I fell?

His words were sincere, despite the way he went about it. Suddenly the conversation in the car and his actions made sense. Not in a normal way. In the fucked-up way that only demons could ever seem to think is something close to logic.

"And after that?" I asked, my cheeks heated but the darkness made me brave.

"Was because I wanted to, and I take what I want. I didn't plan that, if that's what you're asking."

"You say you take what you want…" My voice trailed off. I was unsure how to go about asking this question.

"Yes?"

"Do you want me because you have to?" I asked. He bristled at my questioning.

"We are equals, Ruby. I don't want you because I don't have another choice. I want you because I just do. It's really as simple as that. Don't overthink it," he replied.

"But what about you being a Horseman? You're not the only one that wants me. Is that because—"

"No, it's not. Our duty as the Horsemen does not

impose some kind of supernatural bond on us to make us want anything. Whatever the others *feel*"—he said it like the word was dirty—"it doesn't come out of a place of duty. We simply want what we want, and right now you have all of our attention." I couldn't tell if this pleased him or if it was bothersome. The same way the dark hid me, it also hid him. I fell silent and leaned against the doorframe as a thought came to me, unbidden and savage as my desires.

What if I wanted all of them?

Now *that* was a wicked thought.

Almost as wicked as the answering smile from the beast within.

ALLISTAIR

I couldn't predict her even if I tried, and believe me, I have.

One moment she is perfectly submissive, making sweet little moans. I loved the sounds that came out of that mouth. Perhaps a little too much. The next minute she fucking bites me and it becomes increasingly difficult not to bend her over the hood of my car. I've started to dream of the latter nightly.

She doesn't know how desirable she is. She doesn't know that I crave her filthy mouth for more than sucking my cock, but one day and one day soon—she will.

She almost fed tonight after I took from her. I could feel it. That tentative soul of hers reaching for mine and I don't even think she realized it. If I hadn't pushed her away, she would have fed and it would have triggered the transition instantly, and neither of us were ready for that. As much as I would love to be the only one to take her through the transition, the timing was all wrong.

We had no way of knowing which half of her would surface, or if both would come forward. Ruby the succubus was one thing...pre-transition she was much stronger than she realized. And that was the better outcome. If the beast surfaced out here in the woods, I would have no way of containing it. Our little foreplay would have turned into a very real game of cat and mouse, possibly ending with her burning down the entire fucking forest.

And still...I almost didn't stop her.

The beast yearns to claim its first mate and she's holding it back. There is almost nothing more that I want, except to keep her safe. That includes from herself.

No matter. She is close. So very close, and when the time comes...

I will be at her side as one of her claimed mates, and nothing in either world will stop me.

CHAPTER 8

A couple of days passed where no one said anything. Allistair didn't comment about our time in the car. Moira didn't comment on how late I was getting home. Rysten didn't ask what changed, or why I went back to normal. Laran didn't comment on how I sent them away, but then Rysten still got to go with me. And Julian...he pretended that there was nothing there when he looked at me, but I could sense a growing attraction fighting his darker emotions every day. I never mentioned the jealousy in his eyes when the others would pick me up, because he never made a move. It wasn't my business to intrude on his private thoughts just because I could read his feelings.

Every day, one of them would ask me if I'd made up my mind about moving. Despite lack of insulation in my house, I always gave non-committal answers. Part of me was tempted, but my independence was holding me back, and for now they accepted that. So it was good enough for me.

I was just finishing up shading on my client's shoulder when I heard the door jingle.

"I'll be there in a moment," I called, setting down the tattoo machine. After three sessions and over eighteen hours, this client's upper back was finished. A beautifully articulate pocket watch was the centerpiece where it all started. I drew the design from his grandfather's pocket watch that was given to him as a child. From there, a pattern of gears and spiral coils developed around it, branching over his shoulder and around his upper arm.

This client was a watchmaker's grandson who had gone on to be a mechanic. I incorporated his love of cars and wrenches and the end result was breathtaking. These were my favorite kind of projects because they were ones that held meaning. I priced myself in such a way that I tried to deter young kids that were looking for their girlfriend's name on their chest or the latest trend in that dated an era. They were easy work, but they weren't fulfilling. Not like this.

"Let me get a mirror," I said to him. The middle-aged man grunted in response. I walked to the other side of the small cubicle and grasped one of my middle-sized mirrors. I held it up at an angle to the man's back so that the reflection in the small one was displayed on the full-length mirror in front of him.

"It's perfect," he said. Moisture gathered in the corners of his eyes, but I pretended not to notice. I went through the motions of bandaging it up while I rattled off the instructions for care. He tipped me generously and thanked me for my work.

As I escorted him around the side awning that separated us from the front lobby, my lungs constricted in my chest. A man with mousy brown hair and flat blue eyes waited for me. I smiled tentatively at him as I gave my client his aftercare sheet and watched him leave.

"Hello, John. It's been a while," I said, leaning against the counter to give off the idea that I was relaxed. When really, I was anything but.

John was Josh's best friend. He was every bit as logical and straightforward as Josh had been...before everything happened.

John nodded and took a deep, exhausted breath. The bags beneath his eyes told me why he was here.

"It's good to see you, Ruby. You look...well." His eyes were carefully trained on my face. I wasn't sure if his words were meant to be sarcastic or kind.

"I am well. What can I do for you today?" I asked, cutting straight to the point. He blew out another breath that I almost thought was a sigh of relief. Maybe it was disappointment. I kept to myself and didn't read into his emotions. That's what always got me in trouble in the first place: the desire to fix them.

I knew why he was here, and there was no fixing this. I only had lies meant to buy me time.

"Josh is missing," he started. Unlike Kendall, there wasn't the conflict of dealing with the crying-girlfriend-but-also-a-sadistic bitch routine. John was just John. He was a simple man that acted without all the ulterior motives.

"I heard."

"Look I—I know you probably don't care. He cheated on you, and you broke up. Then he got obsessed and started acting all crazy—I mean, I'm sorry, Ruby. I'm sorry for all the shit he did. I told him it was wrong, but he didn't care. He just lost it...but he's missing now." He swallowed hard and it pulled at my heart strings. "You have no reason to care. You're probably thrilled, and I wouldn't blame you. Not after the things he's told me, but you gotta understand that deep down, he's not a bad person. He's just...human."

Human. Somehow it always comes back to that. I didn't blame John for what Josh did any more than I blamed myself. They were all the same. As if the admittance of flaws was inherently a human trait and an excuse for being a monster.

I wasn't angry with John, but I think I was finally starting to get what Allistair meant.

They were human, and I was not.

With my heartstrings pulled taut, I cut them away. Severing myself, not from humanity per se, but from all notions of being something I'm not.

"I don't know what to tell you, John. I get that you're his friend, but he did some really bad shit. I don't know where he's at, and I don't want to know. I just wish that everyone would leave me out of it and let me heal." My words were half-truths and full-lies, but they did the trick. John nodded in understanding and started backing away to leave.

"Of course. I'm sorry, I shouldn't have come. I just—" He stopped and took a deep breath. Grief etched every line of him, and Josh had only been missing six days. That fucker didn't deserve a friend like John. He didn't deserve to be missed. I told myself that when I ordered Rysten to kill him and I would continue to until the day I died.

John stopped at the door and turned back.

"I'm sorry for everything. I feel like I should warn you: Kendall is saying a lot of things right now. She's got pictures and videos; god knows what else. I don't know what happened, or if it even has anything to do with you. I hope for your sake it doesn't." That was the last he said to me before he walked out my door.

I waited until I saw his car drive away before I made any move to leave. With Moira off for the afternoon, staying home to deal with the window, and none of the guys lurking in plain sight, I could never be too careful.

I bundled up in two sweatshirts before grabbing my purse to brave the cold. Today the skies were a mix of cerulean and arctic blue: colors so vivid and striking when placed in a cloudless sky. It was the first day this week that rain, slush, or sleet wasn't coming down on us. I was going to make the most of it.

I locked up shop and traveled a few blocks down. The wind howled as it funneled down alleyways carrying dead leaves and bits of loose grit. The painted shops and side streets were one of my favorite sights in all of Portland. Antique stores, old books, art galleries, and more. On the streets in front of them, musicians dotted the block, playing a range of instruments—usually with such skill that they put big name musicians to shame. Further proof that success is not always equated by talent or capability.

At the end of the block, food trucks sat around the perimeter of a square, packed so close together that some of them didn't even have room to fit a person in between. The smell of fried fish, gyros, eggrolls, and tacos filled my nostrils as I inhaled deeply, my mouth watering as I waded through the dense crowds of people to a truck on the other side of the square.

Someone was just walking away from the counter when I walked up to my favorite Thai food truck in town. The woman taking orders smiled down at me.

"It's been awhile. What have you been up to?" she asked me.

"Same ole', same ole'. Business is booming. Makes it hard to get away from the shop," I shrugged. The lie fell easily from my lips and she nodded in understanding.

"Will today be your usual, then?"

"Yes, please." I paid in cash and went to stand on the other side of the sidewalk while I waited for my food. People of every age and ethnicity continued to pass by. Today was a particularly busy day given the number of people out and about with their kids. Across the street there was a park made for sitting. Most people took their food there on days like today when the weather was nice. Parents let their children run around and chase the pigeons. Men and women out for a run would take their dogs through and stop for a short break. Even college students congregated around the concrete steps, books splayed open and headphones on.

An itch ran across the back of my neck. Something about this picture wasn't right. The kids, the parents, the dogs, the people: they were all fine. I couldn't tell what it was, but something just struck me as odd. It was almost like...

It was almost like I was being watched.

"Ruby!" The girl at the counter called out. Just as I moved, I finally noticed it in the periphery of my vision.

At a distance, it was hard to tell. They wore non-descript clothing and a black hoodie. Underneath that hood, I could have sworn I saw an eye watching me.

Red as a ruby.

I grabbed my food and ran back to my spot to see if I could get a better look.

Whoever it was, they were already gone.

CHAPTER 9

I left the shop earlier than usual on Friday, making sure to lock the door and check my surroundings as I went. No one had shown up since Allistair dropped me off and I wanted to get home while it was still light out. I was feeling paranoid after my sighting yesterday and the beast was back to shifting restlessly.

Perched on my shoulder, Bandit clung to me as best he could through my many layers of clothing. The cold was bone-deep and the wind was brutal. Above me a storm was brewing, staining the skies an ominous shade of Cimmerian. The forecast on my phone called for snow, but if the ground wasn't cold enough, it would be slush by morning. I mentally made a note to wear rain boots to Martha's tomorrow as I got in my car.

The engine cranked up groggily, but faithfully stayed running once it was on. My car liked the cold about as much as I did. I flipped on the heater and pointed to the dog bed I put in the passenger seat. Bandit dived from my shoulder to the plush bed. He curled into himself, purring when the heater finally warmed up. I rolled my eyes and pulled out of the parking lot.

I stopped at Little Big Burger and got dinner through the drive-thru. I proceeded to spend the rest of the ride home trying to keep Bandit away from my food. Damn raccoon didn't care that I was driving or that it was *my* food. No, he wanted my fucking truffle fries something fierce.

I gave him one and snatched the bag away, ignoring the chitters of protest he gave me whilst cramming bites of fried goodness down his throat as fast as he could. You would think I was going to steal the single fry I gave him by the looks he gave me.

"Unappreciative trash panda," I grumbled to myself as I pulled in the driveway. I swung my car door open and Bandit jumped through it, racing up to the front door with half a French fry hanging out of his mouth.

It only took him three seconds to start screeching because I wasn't fast enough for his liking. I cursed under my breath as I approached the front door, guarding my dinner from the likes of him. I knew this little game. As soon as I opened the door, he'd make a move for my food, damn near tripping me and harassing me until I dropped it.

Not this time, furball.

I turned the key and swung the door open, wrapping both arms around my bag of food like a linebacker with a football. Bandit scurried inside to escape the cold and I followed.

"Interesting decorating you have here."

The food tumbled from my hands and Bandit let out a screech as he scurried up to stand on my shoulder.

"What are you doing in my house?" I asked, a sliver of the beast inside peeked out at the she-demon from Voodoo Doughnut. She was almost the same as I remembered her. Pointed teeth. Painted claws. White hair with pigtails that looked like they were dipped in purple.

"I'm paying you a visit because we need to talk...*without* your bodyguards present." She gave me a cheeky smile and the beast surged forward.

"Speak." My voice turned cold as Death. Stark as Famine. Rageful as War. Unforgiving as Pestilence. The unknown she-demon cocked her head, a flicker of fear entered her heart. It was only an ember, but an ember was all the beast needed.

"Do you remember when we met, and I asked you about the demons who died outside the club?" she asked slowly. The beast did not reply and I continued to stare at her stone-faced. "I am searching for the rogue demon that caused their deaths. He belonged to my master. That same demon is following you."

She stared at me, waiting for some kind of reply. She was dealing with the wrong Ruby if that's what she wanted, and she went about it in the worst way. The beast cared for very few, and even then, it wasn't out of some notion of love. It was possession and desire. With all others, there was only one type of feeling that could even be considered an emotion, and that was rage.

"Do you have a point you wish to make?" the beast

asked. The she-demon did not appear to harbor ill will, but she broke into our house. That was reason enough to not recede until she leaves.

"I would like to work with you to lure the rogue out," she said, not sounding nearly as confident as when I'd walked in.

"Not interested."

"What do you mean, *not interested?*" she asked. Her white brows drew together as she glared at me. I didn't want to be involved. The Horsemen would figure out how to deal with the imp, or she would beat them to it. It didn't particularly matter to me, so long as he stayed out of my life.

"I do not trust you. There is something you are not saying. Leave now, or die," the beast snarled at her. The she-demon turned ashen and pursed her lips.

"You'll regret this. I have information," she said quietly. The beast didn't give two fucks. I reached my hand out and snapped my fingers. Blue fire came to life.

Holy shit.

I started to panic a little bit and attempted to surge forward and put the fire out. She was firmly in control and had no intentions of stopping until the other demon left.

"All things come with a price. I'm not willing to pay for spoken half-truths that will likely find me dead. Leave." The final word was an order from the beast, but a plea from me. I wanted her gone before my other entity decided to burn the rest of my fucking house down along with her.

She took one look at me, snapped her mouth shut, and walked right out my front door.

We watched her through the newly installed window as she turned her face skyward. The clouds opened and rain began to pour down in heavy sheets. She stood there for what seemed like forever.

And then she disappeared.

The fire in my hand extinguished as I got shoved back into my own body. The beast receded quietly and did not argue for the rest of the evening. I cleaned up my dinner from off the concrete. By the time she left, it was already cold. All that remained of it now was the grease smudges left on my barren floor.

Thirty minutes passed where I debated leaving to go get more food, and a space heater while I was at it. I had my mind made up when someone knocked on the door. I grabbed the baseball bat out of my closet and went to answer it.

"Who is it?" I called.

"Your favorite Horsemen," Rysten called back. There was a thud outside my door. "I brought company and food," he continued. I put my eye to the peephole and grinned at what I saw. Rysten had a hand to the door frame, relaxed as could be. Next to him, Julian stood, stoic and aloof. He held a paper bag in one hand and eyed his brother warily. I put the bat behind the door and swung it open, plastering a smile on my face.

"There you are, love," Rysten smiled warmly. He moved in front of Julian and led me through my own living room and into the kitchen, leaving his brother and the food at the door in the pouring rain.

"You mentioned food." I turned to eye the paper bag as Julian came striding into the kitchen. He wore his impassive mask well, but displeasure radiated from him in waves.

"Your house is freezing," Julian commented while he unloaded the bag.

"It's a little bit better with the window replaced," I said lightly.

"And the living room insulation?" he asked. A bit more forceful than asked really. Not quite a demand, but his underlying point was clear.

"Moira met with them yesterday. We were going to discuss our options over the weekend," I replied stiffly.

"If you moved in with us you wouldn't need to worry about it," he continued. I narrowed my eyes at him and stuffed my tongue in my cheek. Before they arrived, I had been debating on texting one of them to tell them what happened with the she-demon from Voodoo Doughnut. Now I wasn't so sure, given that Julian would just use it in his arsenal of reasons why I should become dependent on the Horsemen, and then just skip out on life and fast forward to becoming the destined queen he so desperately wanted me to be.

Rysten ran a gentle hand down my arm and motioned to the rickety table before us. "Why don't we eat, and we can discuss you moving in later?" he suggested. Julian's jaw did that tick thing it does when he's angry, but we all took our seats and pretended that the tension wasn't palpable.

Rysten reached forward and started removing tops from dishes. My mouth watered instantly as the scent of Shrimp Pad Thai fell over me. "Is that what I think it is?" I asked, reaching for the tasty dish.

"Shrimp Pad Thai, number five, from E-San," Rysten smirked. It reminded me of the smile Allistair had when I told him the tea was perfect.

"You're the best," I crooned between mouthfuls of steaming noodles. As soon as the words were out of my mouth, whatever storm was brewing within Julian became infinitely worse.

All four of the Horsemen have the problem of wearing their power too loosely. I have grown to realize that is partially because they can't help it. In the same way that my beast fights me, their power is simply too much to be easily contained. The fact that Rysten attempted to for my sake was sweet, and it was honestly somewhat frightening that he could even accomplish it. The other part of them, I believe, is that they have done it for so long that I don't think they notice it.

Unlike me, who was new to this whole power dynamic, they have been around for thousands of years. They've never had any reason to contain it.

The problem was that it bleeds into me and colors my own perceptions. Much like it was doing right now.

I clamped my mouth shut to keep from saying anything, but the damage was done. My good mood had gone sour. I placed a lid on my dinner and pushed it away. My elbows rested on the table as my hands fell together in a steeple. They both set down their forks and regarded me curiously.

"Something wrong, love?" Rysten asked. The shuddering in my heart intensified. Blood roared in my ears.

"Do we need to talk?" The question was aimed at Julian as a not-too-subtle hint for him to either say his piece or calm the fuck down.

"Have you been outside this afternoon?" Julian responded. Was he purposely evading my question? He can't be so stupid as to not see what I was getting at. Maybe him changing the topic was his way of saying he'd cut the shit out.

"I came home right after work." They locked eyes, and it didn't take a mind reader to tell that they were engaged in a silent conversation. "Did something happen?" I asked slowly. Rysten sighed and turned away from his brother. He reached behind him, into his back pocket, and withdrew a folded-up piece of paper.

"What's this?" I asked. Rysten handed it over to me silently.

"Open it," Julian said.

I ran my fingers over the fraying edges and slowly unfurled the single sheet of paper. Dread formed in my gut when there was nothing left but the final unfolding and my fingers stilled.

What could possibly be in here that would make them both so melancholic?

Only one way to find out.

I opened the paper.

And instantly understood.

In large, bolded black letters: **Justice for Josh**.

Accompanied by a picture of his face.

But that wasn't all.

My face. And the picture she showed me several days ago. That picture had a date and time stamp and a website claiming to have more information underneath.

She all but said I outright did it.

Whatever *it* was.

My fingers brushed over the creases in the paper, committing them to memory. I didn't say anything while I allowed myself time to process this. Eventually I muttered, "Where did you find this?"

"She has them up all across town," Rysten replied softly. I didn't want to see the pity in his eyes, but it was too late. Just as much as blame and self-loathing existed in Julian's. Maybe I had misread Julian. Maybe not. Right now, it didn't matter either way.

"Am I going to be arrested?" I asked, the thought should have scared me more than it did.

"No. Allistair has already taken the liberty to speak with the police on your behalf. You have an alibi, and because these pictures were illegally obtained, they aren't admissible in court." Rysten knew just the thing to say. He was so sweet. So kind.

Maybe that's why it was what he didn't say that I heard the loudest.

I won't be arrested, but there is going to be blood to pay for this.

"How did she even get this picture?" I continued. Ask

questions. Get answers. That's all I needed to do right now. Just one step at a time.

"We don't know yet. I've currently got a program running to hack into the club's security system and see who accessed this video tape," Rysten said.

Again I nodded, because nodding was better than crying. Nodding was at least doing something. It meant I was at least trying to get answers and keep my life together.

Crying meant I was falling apart, but these people... these *humans*—they weren't worth falling apart for. Josh was dead. The damage was done. Yet somehow, it always came back to me paying the price.

There is always a price. Isn't that what the beast said?

Was this my price for getting even? For choosing to end my own suffering? For making the choice to not be a victim, but instead a survivor?

Whatever heartstrings I had left had been severed when John came to me. All that was left was the shallow beat of my own heart, the strength of my own limbs, and the fortitude of my mind to continue forward.

To survive.

My fingers wrapped around the paper, crushing it into a ball. My beast called upon the fire in my veins, and blue flames sprung to life. The paper blazed a brilliant cobalt blue, and then it was gone, leaving nothing but obsidian ashes behind. I rose from my seat and dumped the handful of ash in the garbage, washed my hands, and took my seat back at the rickety table I bought from Goodwill three years ago.

I reached across the surface and unclasped the plastic top. The scent of Shrimp Pad Thai was no longer as appetizing, but I didn't care. I was going to eat every damn bite.

Because for the second time that week, I made the choice to not let this define me. The choice that it will not break me. The choice to not be afraid.

I know who I am, and Kendall can paint this however the fuck she wants.

I was done caring.

CHAPTER 10

I was ripped from a dead sleep by Moira's ring tone, "Fergilicious."

"What?" I croaked. My mouth tasted like dragon's breath.

"Don't come into the shop today."

I bolted upright. "Why? What happened?" I asked, kicking my feet out of bed. I flipped the speaker phone on and set my phone on the nightstand while I dressed in a hurry.

"Kendall happened. I'm being serious, Ruby. Don't come in. You don't need to deal with this shit," she sighed into the speaker. Moira didn't wait for a reply. The line went dead.

Fuck that. I was not sitting at home and making her deal with everyone like I was some fragile flower. I was Ruby Morningstar, damnit, but today the world could call me karma.

I brushed my teeth and fed Bandit in record time

before running out the door, only stopping to see if my shoes matched after I was in the car. My fingers shook as I gripped the steering wheel.

I took a deep breath. *You can do this.*

I was pulling out of the driveway within three minutes of the phone call. Halfway there I felt like I was getting stopped by what seemed like every red light in the fricken city.

"For fuck's sake, change already," I growled. My complaining didn't make it go any faster. After another ten agonizing minutes in my car, I was finally pulling into the lot behind Blue Ruby Ink. Despite the cold, my palms were sweating as I pulled the key from the ignition. I thrust the door open and raced down the alley, not stopping to catch my breath for one second. My heart pounded in my chest as I ran towards my store, stopping short when it came into view.

I wasn't sure what I expected to find, but a mob of protestors was not it.

Fifty or sixty people were gathered out front, screaming terrible things at Moira as she attempted to rip all the flyers away from the glass wall. These weren't just a few flyers either. They lined every inch of the front of my store, stuck to the glass by rain. More sat at her feet, forming piles of mush at least half a foot tall. The crowd screamed nasty things at her. Called her a murderer and whore.

And right there in the middle of it, was Kendall.

Her white blonde hair was damp from the misting rain. She was dressed as the proper lady with her dress and sheer hose, despite the freezing temperatures. From this angle, I couldn't see her face, but I could imagine the smug smirk on her lips. Or maybe it was the crying girlfriend that showed up today.

I didn't care.

Beside her stood a woman with a microphone. Not a megaphone.

That's odd. Why would she have a microphone? Unless...

A man stood a couple yards back with a massive video camera mounted on his shoulder. A news reporter. She was fucking interviewing with a news reporter, telling the world how I killed Josh. Or kidnapped him. Or tortured him.

Honestly, after everything both of them have put me through, I wish I'd tortured him a bit longer. I wish that I had been the one to burn him alive. If I was going to be blamed for it, I may as well have committed the crime.

Despite all, that wasn't what broke me.

It was when a someone threw a rock.

They didn't throw it at my store. Oh, no.

They threw it at Moira.

It was like the diner again, on the day that started it all.

Except this was a thousand times worse. This time it wasn't just my rage. It was the beast's rage I channeled as well.

"They must die. Nobody hurts what's mine," she seethed.

"No. We won't kill them. That's too easy. I have a better idea," I told her. My feet were sure and steady as I approached the rallying mob. I completely walked around it and right up to Moira. I threw the door open, feeling the crowd behind me start into a frenzy when they realized I had arrived. My best friend looked at me with tears in her eyes.

"I'm sorry," she whispered. I pulled her with me inside and locked the door behind us.

They have no idea who they're messing with.

If I was a different kind of demon, I would kill them all and be done with it. That was what my dark entity wanted after all.

But I wasn't a different kind of demon.

I was Ruby Morningstar.

And they would not break me.

I guided Moira into my office and motioned for her to take a seat in my chair. She wobbled sideways and all but fell into it as the shock set in. In the other room, I grabbed a bottle of water and brought it back to my office, uncapping it and setting it on the desk in front of her.

"Drink it," I told her as I got down on my knees. Behind my desk I kept a safe. Most people would think that was where the money was, given that I was paid in cash quite often. Actually, it was where I kept a list of things in case of emergencies. One such emergency was in case we were ever robbed. I kept the money in an account that Moira managed, but the robbers didn't know that. Like I'd keep that kind of cash around.

"What are you doing?"

"What I should have done the first time she crossed

me." Moira didn't say anything when I placed the gas mask over my head and grabbed a small tank from the safe. I slung it over my shoulder and hauled myself to my feet. I placed the taser in Moira's lap and closed the office door firmly behind me.

"I'm going to need your help for this to work," I whispered.

"Make them pay."

I unlocked the door and stepped outside. People were already backing away, but not Kendall. Her back was to me, still interviewing on camera. She wouldn't know what was coming until it was too late. I smiled faintly beneath the mask as I set the tank down a few feet from the door. Two or three broke away from the crowd in a vain attempt at running.

The beast and I laughed together, because we didn't need a switch or a trigger.

We were the trigger.

My eyes flicked over to the container, no bigger than a loaf of bread.

And then it exploded.

My ears rang with the start of a bad Archer joke about tinnitus. Just like the beast told me, she set it on fire, but no more. She was giving me the chance to take my pound of flesh in the way I wanted to, and for that, I thanked her.

Dust and debris mixed with the particles of chloroform as the light mist carried them far and wide. One by one the rioters dropped like the dead. Falling flat on their faces. It was a terrible sight. Bad in a way that was almost beautiful. I stood amongst them with my gas mask on, rain dampening my sweatshirt, my aged converse sneakers soaked to my ankles from the puddles I ran through in the alley.

It was a monumental moment for me as I stood in this place in-between. Me versus the world. Isn't that the way it's always been though? I was born a demon with two sides and raised a human to hate both of them. Oh, how the world loved irony.

I waited in the rain for every single person in the lot to drop. The cameraman was the last to go, and I looked forward to watching the footage as bodies dropped around, standing against them like the murderer I was.

If I wanted them dead, they would be. It was as simple as that.

No amount of explaining would ever earn back my reputation. Not after this. I acknowledged that as I walked forward, ignoring the squelch of my feet in the water clogged shoes and squishy socks. Leaning down, I turned the recorder off and removed the media card. Bringing my foot down on top of the machine as I did.

Honestly, my foot did very little, but it made me feel better.

I pocketed the card and turned to Kendall.

Her blonde hair was splayed across the dirty concrete. The ends were stained black and her clothes were speckled with mud, but she was otherwise unharmed.

I took a deep breath through my nose, inhaling the

dust and mildew that clung to the mask. This was it. The moment I made my mark.

"*They hurt Moira*," the beast reminded me. That was all she needed to say for me the grab the girl's feet and start dragging her inside.

It was going to be a long day, and I was just getting started.

THE SKIES LET OPEN SOMETIME that afternoon, releasing a downpour that caused anything further than three feet away to fade into the nothingness. It was nice, having a small piece of quiet while I worked. I suspected it would not be the same after today, but I could worry about that tomorrow.

For now, I was out for revenge.

And I'd come to collect.

Moira sat beside me on her favorite barstool, biting her nails as she watched.

"There's no going back. You know that, right?" she asked me for the seventeenth time. I nodded my head, as I brought the tip of the of the tattoo machine to Kendall's face.

She had spent nearly two months torturing me for something that wasn't my fault. Most people would say I should be the bigger person. I shouldn't respond. Just call the cops and let them deal with it.

Here's the thing about that.

People like Kendall, they don't care about the rules

any more than I do. Her family has the police in their pocket. She's been playing this game with me for long enough now that I realized she had no intention of getting me arrested. If I were arrested, then suddenly all of it goes away. She no longer has someone to blame, and without someone to throw under the bus, how could she possibly continue to play the victim?

The simple answer is, she can't.

She needs me. She couldn't continue to harass me, to start riots, try to pin a death or disappearance on me that she knows nothing about if I suddenly didn't exist. Because if she did know something about it, she wouldn't be here right now. She would have torn every flyer down herself if she knew what actually happened to him, because no one, not even her, would risk her own skin if she realized the things the Horsemen would do to people who hurt me.

Josh got what he deserved.

And now Kendall would, too.

I was going to give her everything she ever wanted. I was going to make her face so unrecognizable between the carefully shaded wrinkles and artificially added unibrow, that people would give her the pity and attention she craved for years to come. She would be the beautiful twenty-something young woman that lost her face in a wicked game.

A game of truths and lies.

A game she should have played better.

A game that I wasn't going to lose.

Not this time.

The creases around her eyes now formed crow's feet, even when she was at rest. Her cheeks were weak and sallow, age spots dotting her face. Her brows were constructed of a blend of white, blond, and browns, meant to not only match but to make sure that even if she had laser surgery to remove it—she would never fully be free. Not until her skin was truly old and wrinkled.

Josh may have died by Rysten's hand, but the world would do well to remember that there are some punishments worse than death. As a demon that grew up among humans, I've studied them long enough to know their weakness, understand what makes them tick, and ultimately—destroy them.

Except I didn't want to burn the world to the ground.

I just wanted to get even.

I placed the machine on the table beside us and dabbed at the fresh ink. Kendall's once youthful face now looked like that of a ninety-year-old woman with a unibrow and wispy chin hairs to match. She would do her damnedest to remove it when she woke and saw what I'd done.

I applied bandages to her face as gently as I would any other client. I even took the liberty of having Moira break into her car so she had a dry place to sleep while the chloroform wore off.

How kind of me.

"Can you help me move her?" I asked my green-skinned best friend. Moira's shaking stopped shortly after I dragged the body in, and the suspicious over-calculating banshee demeanor was slowly setting back in.

"I can't really say no. We've already come this far," she sighed dramatically. "Just so we're on the same page: you're the crazy one. I may scream and shit, but I've never done anyth—"

"She overstepped today, and now I'm making sure that she never even thinks about it again. Call me crazy. Call me spiteful. I don't care. I am what I am, and I'm not apologizing anymore." I shrugged my shoulders and leaned back against the low back of my chair. My back let out a series of successive cracks and I groaned in relief.

Warm arms wrapped around my shoulders, drawing me into a tight hug. I tried to open my eyes, but the mass of dark green hair blocked my vision.

"I'm proud of you," Moira said against my hair. Her voice was muffled and raw, with what I suspected were tears that she was trying to hold back. "Now let's go move this bitch before she wakes up."

I cracked a smile for the first time in days. Despite it all, I'd done exactly what I said I would. I didn't break. I didn't crawl. I rose up to the challenge and I'm pretty sure I just beat her at her own game.

Moira and I pulled apart, and I pretended not to notice the moisture in her eyes while she subtly wiped it away. "You know, I kind of hate you for making me cry," she muttered. I chuckled under my breath.

"Is that your way of saying you want the arms?" I mused, rolling the tray that held all my equipment out of the way.

"And risk her flipping out and biting me if she wakes up? No thanks." Moira walked to the end of the cubicle and grabbed Kendall by the ankles. She didn't stir.

"Ready?" I asked, taking both wrists.

"Ready." We heaved her off the table and started the slow trek towards the front door. She was surprisingly heavy for someone so slim. It couldn't possibly be because she had anything upstairs. Must have been the boobs.

We finagled our way around the front door without dropping her, although I did *accidentally* bang her head a time or two on the way out.

Her car was a good fifty yards away, which was fine and dandy if not for the rain. Fortunately, I planned for that and had removed my sweatshirt to wrap around her face. Hopefully she wouldn't suffocate in the ninety seconds it took us to cross the parking lot.

Wind and water hit me simultaneously, and my chattering teeth turned into an all-out symphony. Rain drenched my thin t-shirt, putting the world's hardest nipples on display for anyone that drove by. Luckily, no one did. I'm sure they wouldn't have even noticed my freezing tits when we were swinging a body back and forth as we made our way to Kendall's car.

I held both her wrists in one hand and yanked the driver's side door open, kicking it wide so that Moira could put her feet in first. I wasn't sure if it was a blessing that this wasn't the first time we'd done something like this, or a sign that we needed to find better, less illegal hobbies.

Wrapping a slick hand around one of her slim shoulders, I shoved the rest of her body in the car and positioned her head upright before removing my sweatshirt. Her eyes were still closed and the bandages still dry. My sweatshirt, on the other hand, was a different story. I didn't even try to fit the slopping material over me. I was more likely to freeze inside it than without it.

"We good here?" Moira yelled over the rain.

"One last thing," I yelled back and pushed the wet strands of my hair away from my face. Moira cocked an eyebrow, and I pulled out the metallic silver sharpie in my back pocket.

"What are..." Her voice trailed off as I leaned inside the cab of the car and wrote a message on her steering wheel. "Oh."

"Oh indeed," I smirked while I capped the marker. Moira slammed the car door shut and let out a wicked cackle.

"You know, Ruby, sometimes I think we were made for each other." She threw an arm around my waist, tugging me close. I slipped my bare arm around her shoulders and strolled back to Blue Ruby Ink through the rain without a care in the world.

It was nice being me some days, and other days it wasn't.

But I make the most of it by choosing to be happy as I weathered the storm.

CHAPTER II

I sent Moira off to run an errand and I closed shop soon after. Now I sat huddled in my driveway, dreading the thirty feet I would have to walk from the warm confines of my car all the way to the living room where I was ninety percent certain that it was below forty degrees inside.

Not that it could get fixed anytime soon, given the numbers Moira was quoted at. We made decent money at Blue Ruby. Not an outstanding amount, but enough to live and go out for drinks once a week...up until Pandora's Box. After today, I wasn't so sure that would be the case anymore.

I'd taken the preventive measures to avoid any trouble with the law by calling in a favor to a friend of mine that was a cop. Really, he owed me one hell of a favor, so I figured this would be where I cashed in my chips. He won't be able to keep me out of the woods forever, but he could at least buy me some time before they came knocking with questions. Still, the damage Kendall did to my reputation was already done. I had set off a tank of gas and knocked people out.

Yeah, business was bound to be booming. Not.

I loved my house dearly, and everything it stood for. At twenty-years old, I purchased it with money I was making from doing tattoos. That may not seem like much to everyone, but it was everything to me. It was proof that I, Ruby Morningstar, a girl that barely scraped by in high school, could still succeed. I didn't take the traditional route and go to college. I supported Moira by putting a roof over our heads while she did.

My life was changing. A lot faster than I wanted it to.

And I wasn't so sure where the house, the shop, or even I fit into it.

Something needed to give if I was going to get through this.

With numb fingers and a heavy heart, I reached across the passenger seat and pulled my phone from my purse. I scrolled through the contacts and hit call.

It rang once.

"Ruby? Are you okay? Where are you?" Oh man, Julian sounded pissed. Maybe I should have called Rysten instead.

"Yeah, I'm fine. Listen I—"

"Where are you? I'm at your shop. There's a horde of humans outside that are waking up and appear to be having some memory problems. No one seems to know why they're here."

"They're—I—I'll explain everything when you get

here," I sighed. "I called to let you know I'm at home, packing up my stuff. Moira and I are going to move in this week."

"Would that have anything to do with what looks like the remains of a bomb that I cleaned up before anybody saw it?"

Well shit. I knew there was something I was forgetting.

"I plead the fifth."

"Mhmm. Pack up. I'm sending Laran over," he replied. The line went dead.

I scowled at the rain outside as I stored my phone and began the slippery walk up the steps. The rain pelted me relentlessly, not giving a shit that I was already soaked to the bone and freezing. The elements were uncontrollable and unforgiving that way.

When I reached the top of the aged wood steps, I noticed that something wasn't quite right. The front door was open just a crack. Like someone had closed it in a hurry, by the latch didn't stick. I wouldn't have noticed at all, if it hadn't moved slightly with every whipping gust of wind.

A month ago, I probably wouldn't have thought anything of it.

Today, I realized that Moira's car wasn't home.

Someone had either been in my house or was still there.

My heart thumped in my chest as fight or flight kicked in. It wasn't really a question for me, to run or go inside, because I had reached the max on my bullshit meter for the day, and I'd hit that about six hours ago.

I squared my shoulders, took two steps forward and brought my foot up, kicking the center of the door. It didn't resist in the slightest as my foot and the wind carried it hard and fast into the wall behind it, slamming with a thud.

My badassery was short lived.

In my haste to get to Moira this morning, I put on the worst possible shoes for dealing with rain and slippery steps. I lost my balance and went sprawling as my feet went up and I went down. My ass compacted hard with the porch, pain spiking through me.

No. No, this was not how this was supposed to go, damnit.

I landed in a tangle of my own limbs with a bruised ass and bruised ego.

"Well, well. Look what the rain brought in."

I squinted through the haze to see two demons staring down at me. They wore cruel smiles; a stark contrast to the otherworldly beauty they had. Like many of demon-kind, it was a harsh loveliness that straddled the edge of horrifying and magnificent.

"Who are you? And why are you in my house?" My voice had just the right amount of uncertainty and distress. I played the part of a mouse well, and part of that was because I truly was terrified. Sweat coated my skin and my limbs shook from exhaustion. I took heavy, labored breaths while my lungs screamed in anguish.

Inside me, something else writhed, but I held her back.

"Look how she talks. So brave for a child," the female noted. Her teeth shone black like cut onyx. Great. Not only are they the condescending types, I'm pretty sure those pointed teeth could do some serious damage.

"Don't antagonize the poor thing, Lydia. Let's just get it inside and do the job," the man sighed. *Do the job? What the fuck was that supposed to mean.*

The chick named Lydia bent and wrapped a claw-tipped hand around my bicep. I frowned, kicking my foot underneath hers. She tried to catch herself from toppling forward, but I swiped a hand across her chest, throwing her to the ground next to me. I flipped my own body across hers, straddling her chest to pin her to the ground, slamming my forearm into her jugular.

"You little bitch," she choked out. I pressed down tighter.

"Who are you?" I shouted.

She smiled coldly and dread formed in my belly. Strong arms grabbed me by the shoulders and tore me away from her. I struggled with the male as he hauled me back into my own house, fighting my own rising panic. I needed to stay calm so I could trick them into giving me answers and not accidentally unleash the beast. That would just end in bloodshed, and quite possibly me burning down a section of Portland.

I'd rather not give the police anymore reasons to arrest me or land myself on the FBI most wanted list.

The man's grip on me didn't ease until he'd hauled

me all the way into the house. The female came in after us and closed my front door behind her.

"Savage little beastie. You surprised me there. I'm going to enjoy this one, Ryku," she grinned maliciously. I gave her my best apathetic look and she cackled.

"Just do the job so we can get paid," the man behind me said.

"And if I want to drag it out?" she said in the sappiest voice, pouting her full lips while she stared at him with a sensual longing.

What the actual fuck?

"I don't know, Lydia...something's just not right here. She doesn't feel like the others." His English was almost perfect, but there was a hint of something foreign in it. I just couldn't put my finger on what...

"Oh? Then what does she feel like?" Lydia said and crossed her arms across her chest. The dark fabric hugged her curves perfectly, and the gesture lifted her breasts in a way that could *almost* be played off as nonchalant.

"I don't know. She smells like a succubus, but there's something else. I've never encountered it before. It just *feels* old. Like ancient magic." I cocked my head slightly as the pieces started clicking together. The woman eyed me suspiciously and I knew instantly that look had nothing to do with their job, and everything to do with my nasty little habit of drawing men to me.

"Well then. Why don't we cut her open and see? The imp said he'd pay us double if we made it hurt." Her words were impassive, but her eyes held a sneer. She reached the holster at her waist and pulled out a knife. This wasn't just any knife. The handle was well-used and worn. If I hadn't seen the flash of the blade, I would've thought it was just another hitman job. But I'd never heard of one that used an obsidian blade with glowing cobalt runes.

Oh no. These weren't just your run of the mill hitmen.

They weren't even demons.

"You're demon hunters," I whispered.

Every one of us had heard the whispers. Demon hunters. Magic harvesters. We knew they weren't a myth. I never dreamed of actually running into one.

"In the flesh," she replied. The woman smiled, lifting her ceremonial blade to twirl it on her palm.

"Sent here to kill me," I continued, swallowing hard. The beast glared at me, silently urging me to fucking hurry up with my questioning. She did not like the look of that knife. Can't say I disagreed.

"The imp paid quite a nice price up front," she grinned.

Yeah, I bet he did.

"Lydia..." the man behind me growled. He was getting impatient. I liked impatient. It made people foolish. Rash. I smiled up at her from my place on the floor. I was outnumbered and without weapons. My knees ached and my arms still trembled, but I was not afraid.

"Did you ever stop to think why he sent you instead of coming himself?" I asked her. It was only in that moment that the gears seemed to turn.

She narrowed her eyes and took a step forward. At that moment, a bloodcurdling scream came from down the hall.

Oh no. Please don't let that be what I think it is.

She raised the knife in defense as Bandit came running down the hallway.

"NO!" I screamed.

Time slowed down. I couldn't focus. I couldn't think. Yet I saw every single thing that was happening. It was sensory overload.

A gun shot rang through the air and my newly fixed window shattered into a million pieces. My reflection glared back at me in fragments of my face.

One moment my eyes were blue. The next they were black.

I didn't even register the change as the beast pushed forward. Only the desire to save Bandit fueled me as he charged fearlessly at this bitch to save my life.

"You should have listened to your partner," my entity snarled.

Admiral blue and navy flames leapt to life at her feet, curling inward, licking at her flesh. Inside, I flinched from the gruesome sight as the fire burned brighter and her skin turned to ash, but the beast looked on without a care in the world. Black craggy creases appeared, spreading up her legs to her torso, then the arm holding the knife, and beyond. Those vicious cracks splintered and widened as liquid sapphire glowed from inside them. Her magic blade fell from dead fingers and clattered against the ground as her body erupted in a plume of crystalline ash.

Bandit launched himself at the ash statue the moment it exploded. He landed halfway across the room, hacking like a maniac while I whirled on the man behind me.

Except... he was already dead.

A bullet wound right between his eyes. How that ended up there, I had no idea. Only that it probably had something to do with the window shattering. Someone shot him, but they didn't stick around for the finale.

The beast took this in within a matter of seconds. Listening for any hint of a beating heart in his chest, even though half his brains and blood were splattered across my living room wall. When no sound came but our own beating heart and Bandit's coughing, she turned to the window in search of whoever fired the gun.

Whoever they were, they were long gone.

The only hint of an answer was the glint of silver too far in the distance.

CHAPTER 12

My living room door flew open and the beast turned with a hand raised to kill.

"Ruby," Laran breathed a sigh of relief when he saw me standing among the remains. It wasn't his Ruby that stared back at him, and after Julian's promise to keep me safe, she wasn't pleased with any of them.

Laran made it six and half feet through the door before his steps fell short. Bandit came up beside him and began tugging on his jeans. He did that when he wanted to be picked up. Was that because he liked him? Or was it because he saw what Laran hadn't noticed? He paid no attention to my raccoon as his eyes fell on me, or my beast, rather. Her intense gaze locked on him like a cat with a mouse.

"So tell me, War. How many Horsemen does it take to protect one girl?"

There was no mistaking it. She was *pissed*.

The only thing that was saving him was that she

considered him hers. We all were in some form or fashion. With Moira and Bandit, it was my love for them that gave her a sense of duty. She protected them for me.

With Laran and the Horsemen, it was something more akin to desire and possession. She owned them, because they were hers. They always have been. They always will be. They were created for us. They were the only males that stood a chance, and the closest thing to a mate we would ever find. Except we had four of them.

"What happened here?" he asked. His tone wasn't subservient, and she couldn't decide whether she liked that or not. It was angrier than Julian had dared get with her, and he was Death. What could War possibly possess that made him feel invincible?

She smiled.

"The answer is none because that's how many of you are around when she needs you," the entity sneered. Laran clenched and unclenched his fists.

Please, please don't get in a slugging match with War. I prayed, but not to god. Oh no, she would not hear these prayers spoken by the daughter of the devil.

She was just as spiteful as him in that way.

I prayed to myself, because here on earth, now that Satan was dead...my beast was the only thing that might possibly listen.

"I didn't know she was in danger. I would have—"

"You would have what? Hurried? Ran faster? Not been so lax in the first place?" The blood rushed in my veins as my heart slowed. Steady, like war drums. My body was gearing up for a fight, but it wasn't me in charge. She had complete and utter control.

She took three steps toward him, closing the distance, desire fueling some of this exchange. It seemed we had little control when it came to them. I equally wanted to kiss them and throttle them most days. She had similar thoughts, if not more detailed.

"I will not apologize because words mean nothing. Only actions." A declaration, but not touted as such. He spoke them softly, but there was nothing gentle about War. Only stark truths that could bite as much as they could heal.

The beast liked him for that. She found the truth refreshing, but not enough to forgive.

"Make it up to me," she demanded.

His dark eyes changed, the color altering from onyx to a shade of deep burgundy wine. The hands at his sides went limp as she closed the last foot between us and rested a delicate palm against his chest. Through the thin material of his shirt, a heart thundered.

"Ruby..." He murmured my name like a prayer. Maybe it was a plea. I was not the one he had to appease, much as he might wish it.

"Did I stutter? Make it up to *me*." The Siberian winter held more warmth than the voice that came out of my mouth. Laran did not shiver or balk. Nor did he hide from her command.

He stayed still as stone when she wrapped my hand around his shirt, twisting the fabric to pull him closer. She could sense the conflict he felt within. A storm brewed with such intensity. A need, want, and desperation to be burned by her. By me. He was not like Julian who tried to cover his wants, nor was he like Allistair who pushed me persistently. He was hot and passionate, and his feelings were as muddled and needy as my own.

His lips loomed before us, and she did not hesitate.

My mouth crashed into his. Hot and fierce. She wrapped my hand around his neck, maintaining an iron grip while my lips parted his. Heat swept through my system like a monsoon, relentless in the things it made me feel while doing desire's bidding.

Laran gripped my waist as he hoisted me from the ground. My legs instinctually wrapped around his waist, his cock pressing into me. He carried me with an assuredness and every step rubbed against my swollen clit. I ground against his bulge while his hands slid from my waist to cupping my ass, digging his fingertips into my skin.

A purr escaped my throat, dark and needy as the beast met him head on and without hesitation. I...I was not in control, yet I felt every movement. Every scrape of my jeans against my clit. Every thrust of his tongue as he tried to consume me as much as the beast tried to consume him. For all intents and purposes, it was me, but without the reservations.

I reveled in it, knowing that my mind would be torn with indecision if it were really me in control. This was so much more freeing in many ways, and the beast knew that.

My back hit something hard and solid, but Laran

plowed through, a thud reverberating as the door came crashing down. In this moment, I didn't care what we destroyed. I didn't care as we slammed onto the bed. He started to pull back, and I ripped the shirt from his chest.

A growl rumbled in his throat as he bit my lip. Hard. Copper and sweetness spread between our lips. He broke the kiss right when I gasped, taking in a breath of chilled air. His hands slipped beneath my damp sweatshirt and skimmed my ribs as he pulled it over my head, taking the shirt I wore with it.

I arched my back into his touch. He was so different than Allistair and his need to dominate. Or Rysten, who was sweet and sought to please me. Not even Julian, who's very essence held a pain that made me want more.

Laran wanted me to burn and to burn with me.

I loosened my hold around his waist, letting my legs drop to either side of him and dangling my feet over the edges. He skimmed his lips over my half-naked body, letting the chill air slap my sensitive skin. Without asking what I wanted or needed, he began tugging at my boots, and made quick work of pulling away my socks and layers of pants. He tugged them free with a growl, and the beast smiled and sat up to watch him.

Bared before him in only my panties and bra, Laran got on his knees. With my legs hanging over the edge of the bed, we were eye level as he reached around and unhooked my bra with a swift flick of his thumb. The straps slid loose over my shoulders, the cups falling away from my breasts to the floor beneath us.

He wrapped a well-muscled arm around my waist

and pulled me to him. His bare chest brushing mine as he consumed me in another passionate kiss. He pulled away to trail his kiss down my neck, taking his sweet time to leave bites as he went.

I wasn't sure what it was with all of them and biting, but I didn't want it to stop.

I moaned inwardly, but the beast made not a sound. He dipped his head lower and took my nipple between his teeth. Pleasure shot straight between my thighs and I ground against him, arching my back to give him better access. He let out a groan of approval and continued his descent while the beast leaned back on her elbows and watched.

Laran's perfect physique was speckled with scars, dark and light. The skin did not warp or edge at an odd angle; it was blissfully smooth, but the stories of his past marked him. Much the same as the red brand that peeked out over his jeans. From this angle, it looked like some kind of knot made of fire, but my attention wavered as he trailed his nose down my chest, over my stomach, and to the triangle of cotton between my thighs.

He breathed in my smell and kissed my sex through the thin material that separated us. I was drowning in sensation, unable to do anything, but not wanting it to stop.

She ground my feet into the edge of the bed, lifting my hips for him to make her intentions clear.

He growled, blowing a wave of heat through my panties and straight to the most sensitive part of my body. My hips bucked once, outside both her and my control.

"Tell me she wants this," he groaned against my inner thigh. My breath hissed between my teeth as the beast stared down at him.

"She and I are the same: two sides of one coin."

"That is not what I asked," he growled as he bit into my thigh. He gripped my panties tightly and ripped them, exposing my puckered flesh, ripe with arousal.

"Please us both and you'll find out," she said, swaying my hips before him.

Indecision weighed on him as he watched the beast flout my body. *Our body.* She wasn't human, and she truly would not give an inch if Laran didn't please her. Maybe he saw that, or maybe his own need was consuming him.

Parting my folds, he blew once over my clit before locking his teeth around it and sucking sharply. The beast purred, fisting his hair in my hand. He shifted lower, moving his hands to my thighs, grabbing me roughly. He spread my legs wider and leaned forward to brush his nose over my skin.

"You smell like you were made for me," he murmured. The beast cocked an eyebrow at him, waiting impatiently for more. Laran growled and twisted his head to the side, sucking on the flesh of my inner thigh. The beast didn't make a sound as my heart hammered in my chest. Laran nipped at the skin with his teeth, trailing down the inside of my thigh, a moan escaping from her lips.

"You're teasing me, War," the beast breathed, her voice unsteady. There was a huskiness in my voice—her voice—that let him know just how much this affected her.

Laran's fingers pressed into my legs as he brought those nips back up my thigh and licked my wet and waiting flesh. He thrust his tongue inside of me without warning, pushing my thighs down onto the bed, exposing my cunt.

My back arched as pleasure drove me to rock against him, pushing my hips more with every thrust and flick of his tongue. Slipping two fingers inside me while he nipped my clit with his teeth, gliding them back and forth as I tightened and fluttered around him. As my body began to shake, he pulled back his hand, sliding his arms beneath me to hold my hips steady and pull me closer to his mouth. My climax built, my body uncontrollably curling forward as she locked my legs behind his arms, shifting my hands from his hair to both shoulders.

Only a moment before it happened I realized what she was going to do, but it was already too late. Laran pulled back only a hairsbreadth, when a burning started in my palms and tore through both our bodies like a wildfire.

The aching pressure and searing pain swirled together, triggering my orgasm as Laran took my clit in his mouth, sucking hard. The beast receded instantly, pushing me forward to scream in ecstasy while my body writhed, pouring pleasure onto the bed beneath us.

The release was long and mind-shattering. I was still

gasping for breath when it stopped, shaking from a bone-deep exertion that didn't make sense. I unhooked my legs from his arms and tried to shift back, but Laran grabbed both legs and pinned them down as he rose to kneel over me. His eyes blazed with a scorching heat that would have turned me on again, had I not seen what now adorned the top of his shoulders.

"Laran, I—"

"Did you want me?" he interrupted. The sincerity in his voice shook me.

"Yes, but—"

"Then don't apologize," he replied.

"What?" I asked, my voice edging with hysteria.

"I know this seems like a big deal to you—"

"It's a massive fucking deal. Look at you!" I snapped.

Whatever desires and things we wanted to say would remain unspoken as we both jumped up when a door slammed at the other end of the house and Julian roared, "What happened here?"

For devil's sake...

I wiggled my way out from beneath Laran in record time, slipping my robe on right as Julian stormed around the corner. He stopped short of the broken door that littered my floor in pieces. I crossed my arms over my chest and stared at the ceiling while silence spread between us.

I didn't look, because I didn't have to. Julian's emotions turned from concerned and desperate to shock laced with anger. The polite thing to do would have been to ignore what happened between Laran and I, let me get dressed, maybe even ask about the dead bodies or blown window.

Is that what he did?

Oh no.

Instead, he said, "Why is War branded with your mark?"

Jealousy did not look nice on anyone, human or demon.

But damn I was good at inciting it.

<h1 style="text-align:center">**LARAN**</h1>

She branded me.

Twin pentagrams now adorned my shoulders, identical to the one between her breasts. Except these were not black, but blue. They glimmered faintly in the evening glow coming from her window. Swirling. Moving in a way that brands normally did not.

I touched the tips of my fingers to them, but the skin was unmarred.

Old magic.

Even older than I.

I swept my gaze across to her, wanting nothing more than to reach out. She gave me the greatest gift that could be bestowed on me. The highest honor.

I was the first mate.

And she felt guilty about it.

Possessiveness and territorialism pounded through me, wanting to pummel Death into the fucking ground for what he was doing. The fucker was jealous it wasn't him. It just as easily could have been if he didn't have a stick up his ass and would just talk to her.

He didn't need to make her feel guilty about it.

I took a step closer and her sapphire eyes flared with heat.

That's it, baby. Come to me.

My mind reached out tentatively, trying to brush against her fragile psyche. She'd yet to display any form of telepathy, but I wish she had.

Oh, I wish she had. The things I was going to do to her once I had the chance...once I got Julian the fuck out of here.

"War!" Julian shouted. It reverberated through my very bones, yet none of us had spoken a single word. I cut my eyes to him.

"What the fuck are you doing? Can't you see I'm in the middle of—"

"She hasn't transitioned yet, you fool!" He never shouted. Never raised his voice. In the eons of our existence, I could think of only a handful of times.

It was the tone of his voice that had ice racing through my veins.

She hadn't entered the transition. Not even after branding me had she entered the transition, but oh, she smelled like it. Time was not on our side, and I just made the situation infinitely more complicated and likely to blow.

Because there was no way I was going to be able to stay away now.

It was hard enough not to run to her and fall to my knees.

To give her everything she deserved.

I was claimed and owned as the first mate of the next queen, and I couldn't even act on it.

Fuck me.

CHAPTER 13

"Well...she was not very happy with you all for leaving me unprotected, and we had a little problem with getting her to comply..."

The beast huffed inside of me, purring like a fucking kitten after what she'd done.

Yeah. Little problem didn't even touch the tip of the iceberg on this one.

"The beast." Julian's jaw did that thing again where it ticked. "She branded him?" he asked.

I nodded guiltily.

Julian said nothing as he glanced between us, schooling his face into a neutral expression. Somehow, I didn't think Laran was buying his show any more than I did, but whatever. He was the one that would barely look at me most of the time, pretending he was uninterested. It wasn't my job to figure his shit out. I wouldn't feel guilty. If I had anyone I needed to feel guilty towards, it was Laran. He was the one I'd branded.

"Well. I suppose we should talk about what happened that led up to *this*." He motioned between me and Laran, a pile of clothes, torn panties and a ripped shirt, at our feet. I bit off my retort about how none of this was happening before they showed up. There wasn't a lot of point. Blaming people got us nowhere.

"Where would you like to start? With the mob I found outside of my shop this morning, or how I was attacked this afternoon when I got home?" I crossed my arms and gave Julian my best neutral expression. His brows bunched up slightly as a small amount of surprise leaked through.

"Start at the mob," he replied.

"Please," Laran added. I gave him a tight-lipped smile and Julian rolled his eyes.

How very human of you, Death.

I gave them a brief rundown of the morning, skimming over what I tattooed on Kendall's face and moving onto the attack. Both Laran and Julian stayed relatively quiet, apart from the occasional outburst of 'why did you do that, Ruby' or 'I can't believe you put your life in danger, Ruby'. By the end of it, they both were watching me with troubled expressions.

"The transition is looming near. Laran should have known better than to—"

"Oh piss off, Death. I'm not in the mood and it's none of your fucking business." With that, Laran stormed out of my bedroom.

"Are you sure about that?" Julian responded, his voice no louder than a whisper.

Oh for devil's sake, can't we all just get along—

A banshee scream reverberated through the house, shattering the window in my bedroom. I clapped both hands over my ears and pushed my way past Julian and into the hallway where Bandit was screaming bloody murder along with her.

"Moira!" I shouted, but she couldn't hear me over her own scream. I shoved into Laran hard, jostling him enough that I caught sight of her on the other side of him. Her eyes flashed to mine and the screaming died in her throat instantly.

Bandit ran toward me and started scratching at my bare legs. I reached down and scooped him up, cradling him to my chest. The ringing in my ears didn't abate, even after she ran and nearly tackled me to the floor. Laran placed a firm hand against my lower back, holding all three of us up as she threw her arms around me.

"I'm so sorry, Ruby. I just saw the dead bodies and lost my shit. I thought something might have happened to you, but I hadn't felt anything and that just made it worse and—"

"Shh…" I whispered. Her fawning over me, while kind, wasn't helping. That damn screech of hers was going to make me hard of hearing one of these days. Not to mention poor Bandit was going to need a visit to Dr. Lummus to make sure she didn't cause any real damage. Oh, he was going to *love* that. She fed him tuna while I rubbed his belly to keep him calm enough for her to be able to give him a simple physical. And when he needed shots? Ha. I was dragging Moira's ass with me for this one.

"What the hell happened here?" she asked, pulling back to glance at the body and pile of ash behind her.

"I was attacked by hunters," I murmured, moving around her. I walked several feet across the cold concrete floors. The footsteps echoed in the absence of furniture, aiding the howling wind outside. I leaned down and picked up the ceremonial blade buried in the ash pile.

"Is that what I think it is?" Moira squeaked. I glanced up at her and took a deep breath. She held her arms crossed over her chest, her forest green hairs stood on end. *Goosebumps.* I blew the glittering ashes off the blade and the runes lit up.

"That depends on how much you believe in ghost stories," I murmured. "I've heard rumors of assassins for hire that can take more than just a life." Moira's eyes never left the knife as I turned it over in my hands.

"Demon hunters?" Moira whispered.

I nodded solemnly.

"Who would hire someone—"

"The imp," Julian answered gravely before the question left her mouth. She stopped short, her face turning a shade deeper.

"He needs to be dealt with," she demanded. She balled her hands into fists. Guilt and outrage battled within her, but in the end, only a creeping helplessness and fierce need to protect me remained.

"He will be," Laran vowed. A gust of wind swept through, carrying the ashes out of the busted window.

He knelt to exam the body: the man shot between the eyes. Julian moved out of the shadows, his eyes sweeping across the dead assassin with nothing short of a clipped fury and cold cruelty.

"You said they looked alike?" Julian asked. I nodded. "That's unfortunate," he murmured to himself. Julian narrowed his eyes on the body, running his fingers across his jaw. He brushed his thumb across his bottom lip but didn't seem to notice. His full attention was on the dead before us.

"Why is that unfortunate?" I breathed, barely wanting to ask.

"Because they were not human, nor were they demons. The dead body before me is Seelie, and your savior knew that." I took a daring step towards the body. In life, his skin was the color of lead. In death, it had darkened to slate; weathered and ashen, like a corpse much older than this one was. His wide eyes were the darkest crystalline white, but held no vitality to them.

Moira's eyes seemed to ask the question that hung in the air.

How?

"Iron," I murmured. "The bullet they used must have been made of iron." The Fae were as ancient as us demons, and while I had never come across one—we all knew the tales. Or at least the whispers of them. The she-demons that ran the orphanages I've lived in were never fond of the stories. They were banned. Written off as legends meant to scare demons and humans alike.

You don't get through this world as a weaker demon

and not listen to those whispers. You never knew what they might say; never knew what information could make a difference in your survival.

The Fae, specifically the Seelie, were rumored to be hunters of all demon-kind. Dark and unyielding in their pursuits, they fought in the name of the first Seelie—Eve.

Yes, *that* Eve.

As it so happened, Eve wasn't the first woman on earth. She was one of two sisters, and there was no Adam. He came much later down the line after Lucifer fell and the worlds were cleaved in two. What was once Eden, became Hell. Her sister, Lilith, remained immortal, beautiful, and more importantly—she got Lucifer. For a time, anyway. Clearly, if I was here, he'd taken up other lovers. As one might imagine, Eve wasn't too happy with her half of the deal. She got stuck with Adam, earth, and mortality. Eve's mission was to bear as many children as she could whilst wiping the world of the unholy divine.

Difficult to hunt demons when you're a mortal. Hence the babies.

"Iron bullets are not something the everyday person carries about. Not even demons." In the back of my mind, something tugged at my memory, but the thought would not surface and make itself clear.

"Whoever saved her knew of the Fae," Laran said gruffly, turning the man's face side to side.

"Indeed," Julian replied. Something unspoken went between them as they locked eyes, no longer than a moment. Maybe I was observant, but I was getting better at reading them. At seeing what was coming next.

"Rysten and Allistair are coming to pick you up and take you back to our apartment. Laran is remaining with me to continue to assess the threat and clean up the damage. One way or another, you will be safe until it is time for you to take the throne."

Take the throne.

My stomach squeezed in painful, taut knots.

Again, the question ran through my mind, unbidden, but sharp as it was true. *If I am not safe here in Portland, what safety could Hell possibly grant me?*

The beast in me snarled at the implications of that statement. She didn't think we should worry for safety. The world should quiver in fear at her wrath.

"How original," I thought dryly.

"Fear is for the weak. It will kill you faster than anything," she hissed back at me.

"A healthy dose of fear means I've considered my options," I pointed out, too pertinent for her liking.

"It means you hesitated."

"Without it, we would not know who sent the Seelie after me."

"With it, you could die."

I grit my teeth, pursing my lips. My jaw was beginning to ache from the tension. Bandit clung tighter to me, letting out a pathetic mewling noise that I'm pretty sure was him complaining he was cold. *Get in line, buddy.*

"Ruby," Moira said hesitantly as she approached me. "I know we didn't want to move in with them, but today was shit. First Kendall and the shop, now this—I mean, I just had the living room window replaced. We can't afford renovations, all our windows are broken, the heat bill is going to be insane this month. I just..." She trailed off as her lips rolled together in a tight frown. Several dark strands of hair slipped free of her ponytail and blew in the wind. "It's not safe for you to be away from them anymore," she whispered.

"I know," I said. Her hands were smaller than mine, with short stubby fingers. It made it easy for me to wrap my awkwardly long hand around hers. They shook from the cold and the declining adrenaline rush.

"It's not safe for you to be here—in Portland. Ruby, I think it's time we..." Her voice broke off as she struggled for the first time to give words to what I'd known since the day the pentagram showed up on my chest.

"I know. That's why I already told Julian that we're moving in with them. We'll need to figure out what we're going to do about Blue Ruby and selling the house, but after today, I think we both know my time here is... limited." I paused, swallowing the lump in my throat. "I'm not ready to go to Hell. It would probably chew me up and spit me back out, but right now, I'm not seeing a lot of other options."

I so wasn't ready for this. Any of it. I don't get that luxury since I inherited not only Lucifer's kingdom, but a swath of enemies as well.

"We'll figure it out," Moira said. I shook my head sadly.

"I'm so sorry you got dragged into this mess. I'll find a way to make it right. We can set you up somewhere nice, and I'll come back to visit—"

Moira threw her arms around my neck, hugging me close. "I've invested twelve years of my life into you. You think I would let you run off to Hell alone to become queen? I want a return on my investment!" she declared. The worry that held me thawed against the coarse laugh that broke through my lips.

It had been a long day, and there will be many more to come. My friend could hold the cops off, but only for so long. My house was wrecked; my reputation going up in flames behind it. I'd branded Laran, even though I'd yet to hit the transition. The imp was still out there, hunting me, as the Horsemen hunted him.

Some days happiness is not easy; it is a choice.

Despite it all—I chose to smile.

JULIAN

The moment my brother picked her up and took her back to the apartment, I reanimated the Seelie and questioned him.

Not that I expected much of anything beyond what Ruby said.

"I asked who sent you," I demanded for the third and final time. I wanted to push the matter and force it, but souls struggle to linger more than an hour. As it was, the Seelie was twitching uncontrollably, fighting to break free of my control.

"I told-d you-u-u," the body rasped. "W-we were paid-d. I n-n-never sssaw the facccce." The body started gnashing its teeth together. If I forced him to stay, I'd be dealing with a zombie. While that punishment would be fitting, I needed to conserve my strength for something else.

"And you were told to make sure she knew it was an imp that sent you?" I forced the soul to stay with us long enough to nod confirmation, at least as much as the dead could. Releasing it was akin to dropping the leash on a dog. It slipped through the body and into the air as a vague outline of the Seelie he had been. The ghost winked at me and I sent it back to the void, letting War incinerate the thing's body.

"Seems odd that whoever hired him would want her to know the imp did it if they were sent to kill her," Laran said over the crackling flames.

"Unless they didn't expect her to die."

"Maybe they just wanted to scare her," Laran suggested.

"Perhaps. What I can't understand is how they would take a job *from* a demon and not kill them instead?" Something seemed off about this attempt. It was both too poorly thought out, and too convenient for it to be what we were seeing. There was more to it, but what more was hard to tell.

"I'll get Rysten on it. See if he can find anything," Laran said. We stood in silence while I waited for the flames to wink out of existence before I stalked across the room and punched him in the face.

"Was that for her being attacked, or for me being claimed the first mate?" War cracked his neck back into place and spat a glob of blood.

"You're a fucking idiot for putting her at risk," I snapped, having to reign it back in so we didn't accidentally level her house.

"Ahh. You're pissed because she branded me, and you think it should have been you." He didn't shout. Why would he when he was claimed as the first mate? He wasn't wrong about why I was angry, but I punched him because he put her in danger.

"Our duty is to protect her. She's now even closer to the transition, and if anything triggers her before we find the imp—or whoever sent these two—all of us will be put in a vulnerable position. Think about how long most demons need for it. Now realize who we're talking about." His eyes flashed, but he said nothing. As he shouldn't. He fucked up big time here.

"She could be stuck in it for *weeks*. That is *weeks* of appeasing the beast. *Weeks* of trading off which one of us will be with her while the others guard. And that's if she only wants one at a time. We have no idea how large her appetite will be given that she is half-succubus."

Oh, but I dreamed.

In the beginning, I could tell myself that she did not affect me. That I was only her guardian and that's all I will ever be. I could blame her bedroom eyes on her succubus nature. I would tell myself her sinful curves and sultry mouth affected all of us this way.

It meant nothing.

Then the beast emerged.

It was not as easy now that she smelled like she was fucking made for me.

I wanted her with a desire so sharp it was painful.

That's exactly why I couldn't have her.

CHAPTER 14

You know that feeling when you have a million and one things to do, you're standing in line at the grocery store, and the cashier is just blabbering away why she takes her time to ring up a gallon of milk and bag of powdered donuts? That's a bit how today felt. Six clients called and cancelled their appointments. Another ten I had to schedule throughout the week to finish up with. What was left of my house was getting appraised in three days and put on the market—we had to have our shit out by Friday. Blue Ruby was being closed down and the lot sold off. And ever since I had branded him, Laran was strutting around like the prized stallion he thought he was.

I wasn't handling any of this. No, I was avoiding it like the fucking plague while I focused on finishing coloring the pepperoni in my current client's sleeve. At the time, I thought it was an amusing request, albeit odd, to have all her favorite foods tattooed on her. I should have realized then how weird this chick was. She's been running her mouth incessantly for the last hour about macaroni and cheese—a staple food that she had requested I make the base of this design.

I was just finishing up the slice that wrapped around her forearm when the bell on the shop door jingled. I glanced over at Rysten, standing guard next to my cubicle. We'd told mac'n'cheese lady he was shadowing me, and she didn't question further. You wouldn't even have realized he was there if it weren't for the occasional looks the client gave him while licking her lips.

"Can you go check on th—" My words cut off at the sound of approaching footsteps. Too heavy to be Moira, too fast to be a client. Rysten wasn't alarmed. He did little more than let an easy smile slip onto his face as Allistair rounded the corner.

"I need a word with you," he demanded. His eyes swept over the situation, but he didn't seem to particularly care I was in the middle of a session. Fire burned in his eyes, a quiet rage that no doubt had something to do with me. I glanced over at my ogling client to see her mouth was just kind of hanging open.

I rolled my eyes. "Let's break for five minutes. Feel free to get up and move around, but don't touch your arm or brush it against anything." Her head snapped up like she just realized she had been staring and nodded sheepishly. I turned to follow Allistair out and both men held smug grins on their faces. I cocked an eyebrow, walking past and *accidentally* brushing up against them both as I went.

I left the office door open behind me and crossed to the other side of my desk before Allistair entered. The door clicked shut softly and I swallowed hard. Taunting him in the hallway didn't seem like such a good idea anymore. Funny that.

I clasped both hands behind my back so he couldn't see me fiddling with them. Why was he here anyway? If this was about Laran...*Shit*.

Allistair didn't seem like the jealous type. But neither had Rysten until Laran apparently started walking around shirtless this morning in their apartment. I got to hear all about that already. Living with them was going to be a real pain in my ass.

"When were you going to tell me?" His voice was soft as velvet, but it was woven into a noose. I shifted uneasily side to side, debating on calling Rysten in.

"It's not like I *meant* to do it..." Wrong. Wrong way to start this conversation.

Allistair's eyes hardened. "How in Satan's name do you mean to tell me—"

"Hey!" I snapped at the tone in his voice. My own temper rose to match. "You said yourself the lot of you want me. It's none of your damn business what goes on when I'm with the others. Hell, if I want all of you—then I'll have you."

Allistair's mouth dropped open and he fell silent. A thrill of victory ran through me, making me brave. I crossed my arms over my chest, letting my smugness permeate the air. Not that it lasted long. Allistair's shock wore off rather quickly and those sinful lips curved into a knowing smile. My own smirk slipped from my face as my lips dropped into a neutral expression.

"What are you talking about, Ruby?" His lips caressed my name. So wicked. Heat pooled inside me, making me stand straighter. Just the way he said my name made my pussy clench. I pressed my thighs together and his eyes flicked down at the movement, his smile growing into a wolfish grin as he took a step closer.

"I..." The words caught in my throat as he took another step towards me, maneuvering himself around the desk.

"You what?" he murmured and took another step, putting him inside my bubble of safety. My bubble of clarity. I couldn't think with him, or any of them, this close. I took a step back and he pursued. Faster than I could react, he grabbed my hips and planted my ass on the desk. His hands gripped me tight, but not painful. Not yet anyways. He used one knee to knock my legs apart and push his way between them.

"I—" I broke off, snapping my mouth shut. I didn't appreciate being manhandled into giving him what he wanted...and yet, with him, I did. I bit my lip hard and swift to clear my mind. "Why don't you tell me what you're doing here. I have a client I need to get back to, and I doubt you are going to fuck me here on my desk."

He dipped his fingers under the hem of my shirt, toying with the skin.

"Be careful with that mouth of yours. I haven't fed in a week, and I can think of *much* better uses for it," he whispered. Cool lips brushed against mine and I moaned against him.

Motherfucker.

"Now, now. Is that anyway to talk to me?" he sniggered. I froze.

Shit. I didn't think I actually said it...

"Fuck off. Either tell me what you came here for or let me finish up this client," I snarled back at him. Allistair took a step back at the same moment the beast lunged forward and wrapped my hand around his shirt, holding him eye level just long enough to utter, "*Mine.*"

Devil fuck her. She slipped back just as fast she came, leaving me to handle Allistair's probing stare.

"She's possessive," he commented.

"So it appears," I replied dryly.

"If she is, then you are, little succubus."

"I branded Laran." The words popped out of me and there was no taking them back. Allistair blanched, schooling his face into an unreadable expression. I didn't need his body language to know the truth. He stood far too close to hide it, and with my own guilt already twisting inside of me, I didn't want any part of him influencing me, too.

I pushed him to move and he stepped aside, giving me just enough room to close my legs and slide off the desk. I avoided his gaze as I stepped away from him, straightening my spine.

"What are you here for?" I repeated, crossing my arms over my chest.

"To scold you for how unbelievably stupid your stunt with Kendall was," he replied briskly.

"There's no proof," I muttered like a sullen child.

"No proof? Did you really just fucking say that?" His voice rose with the cold arrogance he seemed to pride himself on. Only I knew his secret. It was all a façade.

"I took the video. Broke the recorder. There's no proof the court can hold me to," I said in my snootiest and most obnoxious voice possible.

"You tattooed her whole fucking face, Ruby. You left a *message*. What was it? 'Now your outside matches your inside?' The only thing saving you is my money and reputation—what are you doing?"

I bent over to unlock the safe where I kept my goodies, angling my body so Allistair couldn't see inside. If he was going to have a conniption about Kendall, he sure as hell wasn't going to like what I kept in there.

"One moment." I reached down and plucked the paper I needed, locking the safe back up again before standing to face Allistair.

"What is that?" he asked suspiciously, motioning to the paper in my hand.

"A signed waiver so she can't press charges." I couldn't hide the smugness from my voice.

"You forged her signature," he deadpanned, ripping the paper from my hands to examine it.

"She ruined my reputation, tormented me about Josh for months, and you know what? I didn't care. It was getting old. I never gave a damn for anyone's opinion but my own and I'm not about to start." I met his gaze with nothing but honesty. "She crossed a line when someone in that mob threw a rock at Moira. I may lose my license. I may get fined. They may even try to put me in jail, but I've already lost this life, and I'll be long gone before the court acts. But Kendall"— I paused, my eyes dropping to the scattered designs across my desk—"she will never be able to forget this. She will never outrun her past. She can try to have it removed. She will be in so much pain and it will never truly be gone; I made sure of that. Every single day of her fucking life she will see the face I gave her when she looks in the mirror. I've killed people and come to think that it was too easy a punishment. Making that person live with the consequences...that's justice."

Allistair did not speak. We said nothing to each other for a very long moment, long enough those five minutes were most definitely up. We simply stared.

It was not a staring contest in the sense that he was waiting for me to break and look away, but in that he was searching for something in me and I think he found it.

I think we both did.

"Consider the legal side of things handled. We still need to discuss what you want to do with the house and Blue Ruby, but I will try to make the transition as smooth as possible." He turned on his heel and made to leave.

"And Ruby?" He paused with his hand on the knob.

"Yes?" I asked. A single word never felt so exhausting.

"Your father would have been proud."

I opened my mouth, but fell short of finding any kind

of intelligible response to that. Allistair didn't wait for one and the door clicked shut behind him.

Given that my father was the devil, I wasn't sure if that was a compliment or an insult. Knowing Allistair, it was probably a bit of both, and I was best not to dwell on it too much.

I still had to survive the week. And it was only Tuesday.

ALLISTAIR

She's so close and yet so far.

Julian is trying to keep us at a distance ever since she branded War. That fucker has been sporting it about, how he was *chosen* first. Of course, now that it's happened once, she's even more careful, holding me at arm's length because she's scared it will happen again.

I blamed him.

What none of them know is how close her and I have come to that, but I put her first and stopped it from happening. War is an idiot if he doesn't realize that he's fucking lucky Julian showed up and stopped them. We can't afford for her to enter the transition right now. Not with the imp out there sending the fucking Seelie her way.

I don't even know how she managed to brand him without entering it. Not only is it unheard of, but it lends more credence to Pestilence's theory. Something happened, and like her feeding, she is holding off.

The problem is that eventually something will happen again, and she will blow.

We're handling a hair trigger that could go off at any moment, over anything.

But at least she thought to forge the girl's signature before I went and paid off the cops and the judge. Funny how little the law was enforced when money was flowing.

I had to praise the forethought she used, and I meant what I said.

Her father would have been proud. She will make a great queen.

Fair and ruthless. I couldn't ask for more in a she-demon that will one day rule.

Which is exactly why I will be standing at her side.

Rysten is hell-bent on being claimed next, but not if I have anything to say about it.

CHAPTER 15

We hurried down the well-lit street, our shoes softly slapping against the wet pavement. A subtle mist permeated the air, making the freezing temperatures downright icy. I shoved my hands in my armpits and ambled towards my favorite restaurant, The Alley Cat. Next to me, Rysten let out a soft laugh.

"You won't be laughing when your balls freeze and you can't make any little pests," Moira snapped, storming ahead of me. I smiled at her back as she tugged her hood tighter and shoved past the drunken group of college kids. A chorus of, 'Hey! Watch it!' followed her as one of the boys fell over sideways into a trash can.

Talk about getting wasted. I sniggered at my own pun.

Moira didn't spare them a single glance as she plowed on, diving into a side alley. I followed after her, ignoring the shouts behind us. They may yell, but no one would dare cause trouble with Rysten standing beside me. Easy-going nature aside, he had a strict no bullshit policy where I was concerned. Only Moira and Bandit were exempt.

It was reassuring, but also a bit patronizing. He was at least considerate in his duties, unlike the other three, who were all their own unique forms of overbearing. Rysten made it feel more like the three of us were just getting dinner. The reality was it was me and Moira, and he had to come along because I can't go anywhere alone. Not anymore.

I treaded carefully across the cobbled street. It wasn't pavement like most of Portland, but instead a layer of rocks imbedded on top of a cement finish. The stones were smooth and slick in the misting weather. Rysten saddled up to me, gently cupping my arm at the elbow to help me keep my balance.

"Thanks," I breathed, pulling my arm away as soon as we reached the steps. Rysten didn't say anything, but I could feel the pleasant warmth that radiated from him. Did he know his hand was like a hot iron against my skin? Could he feel the way my body reacted underneath three layers of clothes?

I shook my head to clear away those thoughts as I gripped the wrought iron railing and ascended the steps. Inside, Moira waved an arm in our direction, beckoning us toward a booth in the back.

"*This* is your favorite restaurant?" Rysten asked skeptically, his eyes swinging from the very plain wooden booths that lined the space to the moving tables that traversed the room. Each one oversaw an aspect in pizza making: dough boy, the sauce guy, toppings, and finally to the oven where it baked into delicious goodness that waitresses would then serve out. The moving tables shifted and turned without managing to hit each other as they created pizza so heavenly, the owner must have been an Italian grandmother in his past life. I smiled fondly at the young man spinning dough high in the air before tossing it onto the next table.

"Yep, and the main event hasn't even started," Moira answered gleefully, a low chuckle escaping her lips. Rysten gave me a sideways glance as I slid into the booth next to her and shrugged innocently.

"Main event?"

"You'll see."

She and I shared a smirk at the scowl on Rysten's face. For once it was *us* who was in on the joke. Oh, how the tables have turned. Quite literally, as the dough boy moved his station in front of us.

"What'll it be this evenin,' ladies and gent?" he asked in a strong New York accent.

"Two large house specials and a pitcher of whatever seasonal draft you're carrying," Moira answered for all of us. His hands were already kneading the dough.

"Got some ID on ya?" he asked. I blanched. Did Rysten even have an ID? I mean, he made my birth certificate and all when I was a child, but what about now? I fumbled with my mini-backpack, giving him a sideways glance out of the corner of my eye. He flipped open his wallet and flashed it at the dough boy who nodded while I dug out my own ID.

"Alrighty then, food will be up shortly," the boy said

with a wink in Moira's and my direction. He moved the cart to another table, and in the process, sent the pizza dough spinning onto the sauce cart while calling out our order. You had to admire the organized chaos that The Alley Cat thrived in. When I was thirteen, I wanted to work here. Then I hit puberty and well...c'est la vie. That's what happens when you're half-succubus. A secluded job was my only prospect after that.

"I didn't know you had an ID." I eyed the wallet he was quickly closing.

"There's a lot you don't know about me, love." He winked as he slid it in his back pocket. "How do you expect us to get around on earth without the documentation humans are so fond of?"

"Well," I drawled. "I kind of assumed you operated around the law and just came and went as you pleased." Our conversation paused when a young woman came up carrying a pitcher in one hand and three frosty mugs in the other. She poured our glasses one at a time and left the remaining half pitcher on the table without a word.

"As nice as that would be"—he paused to take a swig of the frothy ale—"we can't do *everything* around the law. Allistair couldn't handle your legal trouble if not for the fabricated scores on the bar that made him a certified lawyer."

Instead of replying, I took a drink of the seasonal draft. Rich and malty, the pleasant notes of vanilla finished with a hint of peppermint as a faint warmth built in my chest.

Much better.

"Should I be concerned about this case with Kendall?" I asked in all seriousness. If Allistair never took the bar…I guess it was safe to assume he probably never went to college either.

"Concerned? Really, love? We started the firm some hundred years ago. If anyone can get you out of your legal troubles, it's him." Rysten assured me, using his hands to gesture. I wasn't the only one the alcohol was loosening up tonight.

"When you say *the firm*"—Moira cut in—"do you mean that all of you own it?"

"Yes, but Allistair handles the actual lawyer business. Don't tell him I said this, but I think he gets a power trip from it. Certainly wouldn't surprise me," he scoffed. I snorted and choked on a bit of my beer. Moira clapped me on the back harder than necessary, all the while eyeing Rysten with interest.

"Why do you say that?" she asked.

"That he gets a power trip from it?" She nodded and Rysten let out a dark chuckle. "Because Famine and my brother have been at odds for control for a very long time. Him being the lawyer meant he was providing for Ruby, and Julian wasn't. I suspect that's half the reason he does it without complaint." He took another long drink of his beer, draining the mug. Moira was more than happy to pour him another one.

She's so thoughtful that way.

The nosy banshee was well aware of what was making his lips loose—and for once, it wasn't me. Right then, a waitress came carrying two ginormous pizzas, and when I say ginormous, I mean literally two feet in diameter. They barely fit on the table around the pitcher and mugs. Rysten drained his again, refilled it, and topped mine off before handing the girl the empty pitcher. We all echoed our thanks as she retreated, looking slightly skeptical we could eat it all. She didn't know the appetite banshees have. They're notorious for eating ungodly amounts of food, and judging by the size of Rysten, I had a feeling she wasn't the only one.

"So, if Allistair is the only one doing lawyer business, what do the rest of you lazy fucks do?" Moira asked, pulling a square off the tray and biting in while it was still piping hot. She let out a freakishly loud moan and the next table over threw us dirty looks. I held up my hands, like I had no part in it—not that it mattered when Moira flipped them off. The woman picked up her toddler and covered the boy's eyes while the baby clapped.

It almost reminded me of Bandit.

"Really?" I asked her. Moira flipped me off, too, shrugging her slender shoulders. For fuck's sake, let's at least *pretend* to be grown ass adults.

"Well, us lazy fucks, as you so nicely put it, do all of the work outside of the courtroom." Rysten replied, watching me with amusement as I dug into the pizza. I folded it like a sandwich before plopping it into my mouth.

"Such as?" I asked around a mouthful of food. Moira sniggered, arching an eyebrow. I glared back as I swallowed the rest of the slice whole and grinned like a motherfucking champ.

Succubus without a gag reflex for the win.

"Nothing all that terribly interesting," he said vaguely.

"You forged my birth certificate and I'm willing to bet you're the one that forged Allistair's bar results," I replied, much soberer than he was in that moment. His hand halted mid-bite, and his sage colored eyes flicked up to mine. Bingo. "So that's your thing? You forge stuff? Documents?"

His lips twitched as a grin fought its way through. "Amongst other things."

"Hmm." I took another slice of pizza, savoring the zesty tomato sauce and hot red peppers. With the winter beer and warm atmosphere, I was right at home here.

"What about Laran? What's he do?" Moira asked, drawing our attention back to her. She'd only been silent because she was too busy eating. Half of the pizza before her was already gone.

"War isn't really one for politics or computers..." Rysten trailed off, picking up his beer right at that moment. The smirk of his lips told me he clearly found that amusing.

"Figures. He's probably the one that beats people up in alleys," Moira shrugged.

Rysten choked on his beer and put the mug down with enough force to muster a thunk from the impact.

Well, well, now...if that isn't interesting.

"That's what he does, isn't it? He beats people up?" I asked him.

"Not so much anymore," Rysten supplied.

"Anymore?"

"Should I be scared to ask what Julian does?" Moira piped up with too much enthusiasm. Rysten threw her a glare as if to say, *don't you dare.*

"Look, love, we built ourselves a name on mostly honest work. We had a few mobsters back in the early days, a drug lord here and there to keep the money flowing. What do you expect though? We're not exactly guardian angels." With that, he drained the last of his mug and helped me finish off our pizza.

Nothing like a last supper before we leave town for you to figure out who you're moving in with. Although, if I'm being honest, it's wasn't all that surprising. They dealt with the Josh scenario too efficiently for it to be the first time. I mean, they're the Four Horsemen—and I burn people alive. It's not like I have any room to judge.

"Ladies and gents, boys and girls, now is the time we've all been waitin' for." The charismatic voice of the young dough boy drew my attention to the center of the room where workers were clearing away tables. He stood on a lone chair, overlooking the lot of us. He wore a Cheshire smile like the grandest of kings. How fitting for what came next.

"These two lovely young ladies will be coming around with pails of spoiled compost for sale. Five dollars a bucket, to crown the fool!" He clapped his hands and a young girl appeared, probably no more than sixteen, pushing a cart loaded with old vegetables and fruits. The eggs always made for a particularly fun show.

"How many?" the girl asked, blushing at the sight of Rysten.

"We'll take four," Moira said, drawing her attention away from the male across from us. The girl pulled the empty trays from our table and moved the buckets while Moira counted out her cash.

"You got a five?" she asked me and I reached for my wallet.

"I've got it," Rysten said, waving us off. He handed the girl a fifty, told her to keep the change, and gave her a wink. The girl's porcelain skin blushed a deep shade of scarlet while she murmured her thanks and moved to the next table.

"How dashing," Moira muttered. I snorted in agreement.

"So what are we going to do with all of this"—his nose wrinkled in disgust—"garbage."

"You'll see," I replied cryptically. Moira cackled, and a tenor of her banshee rang through, making the buckets warble. I clapped a hand over her mouth as her eyes grew wide.

"Did that just…" she said around my hand. I pulled it back for her to speak freely.

"Yep." I took a sweeping glance around the restaurant, but no one noticed. No one apart from Rysten, who watched us silently with his brows drawn together, a slight pucker formed between them as he ran his fingers over his jaw.

"Interesting..." he murmured. I opened my mouth to ask him what he was talking about, but the dough boy chose that moment to get started.

"Alrighty, listen up!" the young man projected, his voice gravitating over us as he called the room to silence. "It's time for the main event. The one night a month that we come together to crown the King of Fools. This. Is. Bad Poetry Night!"

The room let out a thunderous applause as people slammed the buckets of slop up and down. Moira and I let out a woot, pumping our fists in the air. Rysten stared at us like crazy women.

"This is what you dragged us out here for?" he whispered in disbelief. I shushed him with a wave of my hand as the boy—now known as the marshal since bad poetry night was well underway—called up the first volunteer.

"State your name and poison, if you wish to be the King of Fools!" the marshal called out, stepping down from the chair. His coffee colored hair reflected the soft lights coming from the ceiling, and his chocolate eyes sparkled with mischief, making him look younger than before.

"I'm Standing Willow," said the man that walked forward. His rainbow beanie slouched sideways, only covering half of his long, greasy hair. He wore a baggy t-shirt with a peace sign on it that did nothing for his thin frame, and his gypsy pants bunched at the waist, poofing out around his legs and cuffing at the ankles. I was also pretty sure I owned that same pair of Chacos he had on, except I only wore them when it was *above* freezing.

"Welcome, Standing Willow," the marshal said. His lips twitched like he was having trouble saying that in all seriousness. The beanie man took up his spot on the chair, clearing his throat obnoxiously before starting.

"Shall I compare thee to a summer's day?" the man started.

"Boooo!" Moira yelled. Rysten turned, stricken, which for a drunk demon, was quite amusing.

"Shhh!" he scolded her. "Can you keep your voice down? That's quite rude."

No sooner than he said it did a chorus of boos rain down from around the room. I wasn't sure if I should be amused or feel bad for the guy. On one hand, the idea was to bring the worst poetry to the table, so maybe he was making a joke of dear old Shakespeare. On the other hand, he looked the type that might take this to heart.

"Thou art more lovely—" And that ended right there as Moira arched around me to throw half of a tomato at him. It flew all ten feet, straight and true, right into his mouth. His eyes went wide and he looked down his nose, mortified at the chunk of tomato half hanging out of his mouth.

The marshal stepped up and circled around the beanie man. "First pie hole of the night. What's he going to do?"

The guy doubled over and threw up, spewing not only the tomato, but a good portion of his dinner. He toppled sideways out of the chair where his friends who put him up to this were waiting. They caught him, smiling through their tear-stained eyes, clearly laughing so hard they cried. He righted himself and looked around, pink tinging his cheeks. Standing Willow, it seemed, did not realize what kind of poetry night this would be.

As a cleaning crew came to mop up the mess, the marshal turned to the crowd and shouted, "Disqualified!"

Moira and I smacked our hands on the table, drumming along with the rest of the patrons while another fool came forward.

"So let me get this straight," Rysten said, talking over the noise. "You come here to listen to people recite bad poetry and throw food at them? Isn't that a bit...demeaning?"

My heart fluttered as it had little spasms in my chest. He didn't completely understand the purpose, but his sentiment was in a good place. Better than one might expect for the Horsemen of Pestilence. But I didn't get the chance to explain to him.

"I told you we should have brought Laran instead," Moira muttered just loud enough for him to hear. Rysten froze for about half a second, narrowing his eyes at her. She arched an eyebrow and motioned to the bucket sitting in front of him. The second fool had just finished her performance and the crowd was going nuts. Meanwhile, Moira was giving Rysten a test.

One it appeared, he was not going to fail.

He grabbed a bell pepper off the top as I leaned over, whispering to Moira, "You're a cunt. You know that?"

She sniggered as Rysten pelted the girl with the

pepper to the head and she swayed in the chair. Her hand reached out to grasp the wooden back as she righted herself and pumped a fist in the air. The crowd went wild, throwing all kinds of spoiled goods, but she held firm and proceeded to the next round.

"Wait—so they *want* you to throw food at them?" he asked dubiously.

"Yep," I said, shaking my head while Moira laughed like a fool. A dark glimmer entered his eye, but that was all he said about it for the next few contestants. One at a time, more chairs were accumulated, and bad poets were tested. Some brought snark, others used humor, and only a few dared use something as overdone as Shakespeare. This wasn't the place or the crowd for it really. The ones who were simply booed and had nothing thrown at them were eliminated. Of the others, only those who could remain on the chair withstood. Not that we made that an easy task. Moira had quite a knack for throwing shit. I probably would, too, if my first foster home had been like hers.

The marshal stepped up and waved his hand in the most ridiculous fashion. Really, I think they picked the kid for this job because he acted the part and the crowd loved it.

"Last call for contenders in this month's bid to be the King of Fools," the young man broadcasted. All around the room people looked to their right and left to see if anyone wanted to join the ranks of the three fools that had ascended to the next round.

"I will."

I turned sharply, my mouth falling open. Rysten rose out of the booth and strutted towards the marshal with unmistakable swagger. His tall stature towered over the marshal, who looked up at him uneasily. Like somehow he knew there was something about this man that he should be very, very afraid of.

"What's your name...fool?" the marshal asked bravely.

"Rysten."

Moira grasped my arm while he made his way to the chair, and I was questioning if it was going to break under him. It's not like they gave them sturdy chairs.

"I can't believe he did it. The pest has balls after all," Moira snickered.

"You keep poking him and he's going to snap."

"I'm counting on it." She licked her lips watching him with narrowed eyes. A hint of something ugly ran through my chest, almost akin to jealousy. The word my beast liked to say most frequently danced on my lips. *Mine.*

Moira cut her eyes at me, cocking her head.

Oops. I think that slipped out.

"Yours, huh?" she asked, her eyes shining with mirth. "Took you long enough."

I opened my mouth, but she shushed me as Rysten began to speak.

"Rubies are red, your eyes are blue. Your soul is like fire, I want to burn, too."

Did he just—

Oh yes, he did.

My heart thundered in my chest, beating wildly with the force of hurricane winds. The world slowed as we locked eyes and the tiniest of smiles found its way to my lips. I don't know what it was that suddenly had me so turned on. Maybe it was the look he was giving me, that dark gleam that showed me there was so much more to him than I knew. Maybe it was the deafening silence that spoke louder than the words themselves...

Or maybe, it was the way that he withstood and did not look away from me, even as Moira threw an eggplant at his dick.

He took the hit with about as much grace as could be expected. His lips twitched in a grimace, but he held firm, standing taller than any of the other fools around him. Even as Moira literally drained an entire bucket, just on him.

She was my best friend, and as lovely, brilliant, and loyal as she was—she acted like a fucking child with the Horsemen, arguing over me day and night. She ordered them around enough, I sometimes wondered if maybe it was her destiny to rule, given how adept she was at telling people what to do.

"Alright, ladies and gents, feast your eyes upon the fools. As they prepare to recite it out, to win your favor! Let's begin."

Recite it out? Really? He couldn't come up with anything better than that? Lame.

He turned to the first girl who withstood getting hit in the head with Rysten's bell pepper, and she preceded to recite some nonsense about a llama and a desert. It was bad, but not funny, and while people booed her, they did not throw anything. She was eliminated.

Next came a stout girl with a Scottish accent that sounded like Hiccup's mom from *How to Train Your Dragon*. She cleared her throat once and said, "Skinny went to take a bath, he never told a soul. Forgot to put the stopper in and slipped straight down the hole."

I let out a small chuckle, but the real amusement was when two small children squealed in delight. People started pelting the woman with food, just to get a reaction out of the kids. She watched them with so much amusement that she didn't see the stale bread Moira chucked her way. And just like that, she came toppling down. Another one eliminated.

They should really make people sign a waiver for this sort of thing.

The next fool stood on a chair closest to me. His baby blue eyes seemed to bounce shrewdly between me and Rysten. A sour feeling churned in my stomach when he smiled. Moira stiffened, wrapping an arm around my shoulder protectively. It was like she instinctively knew what was wrong as the boy opened his mouth.

"Roses are red, ready to pluck, I'll pick you up at eight thirty, be ready to..." He left his poem open ended, puckering his lips at me slightly as he smiled. The room once again erupted in boos as they pelted him with food. Moira made a point of trying to knock him off with a couple well-aimed grape tomatoes for the eyes. Bastard held on tight and winked at me while he was at it.

My lips thinned into a neutral grimace as I looked to

Rysten. My heart stilled in my chest at the way he eyed the human on the other chair. The guy's face went stricken as a sheen of sweat broke out across his skin. He opened his mouth to say something, but instead, all that came out was the loudest fart I have ever heard in my life. The room went silent and Moira threw a tomato, hitting him square in the face. He toppled off the chair and caught himself with his back towards me. I then realized it wasn't a fart.

Those were shit stains spreading across the seat of his pants.

And the smell...

"I think I'm going to be sick," I told Moira, pinching my nose. The guy looked around as people sat wide-eyed, shaking with silent laughter, pointing fingers in his direction. His eyes skipped over them and he took off straight for the bathroom. Not even looking back when the marshal choked out, "Eliminated! Aye—can we get some air freshener up in here?"

Workers scuttled out from the corners of the restaurant where they'd hid among the crowd to laugh and cheer with us. Several people started sweeping up the food off the ground, and the girl who had brought around the buckets of vegetation earlier came forward with a crown in hand.

A paper crown to be specific, like the ones you get at Burger King.

"I crown thee, Rysten, King of Fools! At least until next month," the dough boy-marshal declared. We pounded our empty buckets on the table as Rysten accepted his crown with grace, or with as much grace as one could while being coated in a variety of rotten and spoiled food.

With the main event over, people started filing out, but Rysten didn't seem to be in any kind of a hurry as he sauntered over to us with way too much arrogance for someone covered in tomato juice. Behind him, out of the corner of my eye, I saw a glimmer of red. An eye that was watching me from the massive crowd departing. I peered around him, wanting to get a better look. But in a blink, it was gone.

Must have been another trick of my imagination. The beer getting to me, making me paranoid.

"King of Fools, eh?" Moira said as we slid out of our booth.

"Every queen needs a king," Rysten murmured, opening his wallet to lay down a hundred-dollar bill. Moira didn't comment as she stepped ahead, getting ready to wade into the night. Rysten followed behind and I watched for a moment, smiling to myself.

"Why have one when you can have four?" I whispered, trailing after them.

RYSTEN

Why have only one, you say?

Ruby, love, I think you've figured it out.

She may have branded War first, but I would be the second. If Julian was intent on ignoring not only his reactions towards her, but her feelings for him, who was I to get in the way?

In the meantime, her beast is pacing. Relentless. It is looking to claim its second mate.

That will be me.

I couldn't stop myself from exploiting the human. He was making her uncomfortable. A good potential mate would not allow that, but humans don't work that way. Particularly Ruby. She would have been upset if I killed him. My blood pushed for it. I only didn't because he wasn't a potential mate. Should another male try and enter the equation while she's so vulnerable...it would go very poorly for them.

I settled for sickness. All it took was allowing the bacteria in his gut to fester and grow.

He would never know it was I who caused it.

Now that Ruby knows what she wants, I have no qualms with pursuing her. And trying to get War in check while I'm at it. She hasn't transitioned. I don't know how. We have already passed the deadline I assumed she wouldn't meet, but she displayed powers that are unheard of for a demon pre-transition.

We needed to find the imp, and quickly, before something triggered her.

Time was running out. She can't hold off forever.

CHAPTER 16

I flipped the sign on the front door. It was such a small act, just another chore at the end of every day that I had to do while closing. But this time was different.

This time was the last time. Blue Ruby Ink was officially closed, and I didn't know how to feel about that. We were one of the newest, but most successful tattoo parlors in Portland. I created this business with Moira and raised it from the ground up. There was quite literally sweat, blood, and tears put into this place and now... it was over.

I already missed it because of the simplicity this life held for me. Here I was Ruby: a half-succubus whose life revolved around my clients, keeping my head down, and eating at Martha's every Saturday.

It was a nice life. Simple.

But I had this predetermined destiny and nothing I ever did was going to stop it.

It didn't matter that I didn't know about it. It didn't

matter how hard I tried to avoid it, tried to resist. I could have been doing any number of things, and it would have ended this way, Kendall or no Kendall.

I guess it was a bit like damned if I do, damned if I don't.

Hell was going to take me either way. I suppose leaving in the next few weeks when it was my choice (and I was still breathing) was probably the smart way to go.

At least that's what I told myself as I dragged my feet back to my office.

There wasn't any point in bemoaning the events that led me here. That would help no one. It would just be a lot simpler if I knew what exactly I was moving towards when all of this settled. Would we just go to Hell and bam—I'm queen? I wondered if I would sit at a desk much like this, ordering people about. Somehow, I didn't think it was going to work like that. Call it a hunch, but the guys were being particularly cagey anytime I asked. That sounded awfully boring anyways, but it's not like there's anyone else up for the job. Except maybe Moira.

At least I'll have her and Bandit. I wasn't quite sure what my ferocious little raccoon would do in Hell, but I wasn't leaving without him, so I guess we were all going to find out. Would that make him a Hellcoon now? I had no idea, but Rysten assured me he would be fine. The portals for Hell transported much more than just demons in and out, and while I'm sure he meant for that to be comforting...all it did was bring me nightmares about what I would find when we eventually got there.

Three knocks at the door made me jump. I turned back just as Moira popped her head in. She took one look at me and her brows drew together, her lips pursing before tightening into a slight frown. "Why are you in here wallowing?"

"I'm not wallowing," I snapped. She arched a perfect eyebrow, slipping through the door and closing it softly behind her.

"Yes, you are."

"Moira—"

"Ruby Morningstar, I have lived with you for twelve years. I know when you're happy. I know when you're upset. I know when something is wrong, and right now, I *know* you are wallowing. Don't deny it. I know it." Moira crossed her arms over her chest, waiting for me to cave.

"I'm not wallowing, Moira. I'm thinking. You know that thing sane people do when making huge life choices?" I quipped back. She didn't seem to find it funny.

"Well, stop it. It's not like we're leaving anytime soon. We only just got the house on the market and we've still got to deal with getting this place cleaned out." She looked around my office like she somehow found it lacking. I lived in organized chaos. Sue me.

"I know it's not the end, and I know we're not leaving yet..." I took a deep breath, looking up at the specks of dust on my ceiling that I've counted a thousand times before. "It's all just moving too fast for my comfort." I shrugged, pulling on my long sleeves awkwardly while I waited for Moira to throw her head back and laugh at me.

"You would be crazy if it wasn't, but that doesn't mean I'm going to tell you not to do it. You've been attacked more times than I'm okay with and as much as I find the Horsemen obnoxious, I know they'll keep you safe." I blinked when she wrapped her arms around my shoulders and pulled me close. She smelled like fresh laundry and a hint of mint. It was a scent I knew well.

"That's surprisingly sappy for you," I muttered into her hair.

"Tell anyone and I'll deny it," she huffed back.

Someone knocked on my door twice before opening it without permission.

"Excuse you," Moira snapped. "We could have been having hot lesbian sex in here and—"

"I know she's straight, banshee," Laran smirked.

"You don't know that," Moira replied testily.

"Yes, I do." His self-assured expression and subtle reminder about his brand made my cheeks heat. He gave me a wink and held the door open, motioning for us to go through. "Still want to go by the house before we head back to the apartment?"

"Yeah, I need to pick up a few things. Bandit's been going stir crazy at night without his pink elephant." Next to me, Moira grumbled in agreement. He's been keeping us up half the damn night trying to crawl under the blankets and nip at my feet for ignoring him. Bastard drew blood last night. Yeah. Now that I think about it, he'll probably do just fine in Hell.

"Is the banshee coming?" Laran asked.

"The banshee has a name, you know," I replied. He

didn't even attempt to look reproachful or sorry. I think he was still a bit salty about Moira ringing him out two weeks ago for pounding down my door. Not that she was really making it any better.

"I'm going to stay and pack up some more," Moira said, waving off the invitation.

"You sure?" I asked.

"Yeah, I'll swing by the house afterwards to load up my car with more boxes and meet you back at the apartment," she said, practically pushing me through the door. I kissed her cheek and headed out with Laran.

Today's skies were a cloudless blue, but the day was already nearing sunset. Across the city, the blue darkened to indigo and violet where the sun was barely touching the horizon. Without the cloud coverage, the air was even more frigid, and my teeth started chattering in seconds.

"Cold?" Laran asked, tugging my hand out of the jacket pocket. I didn't complain. His hand was toasty warm, abnormally so.

"How are you not?" I asked, eyeing our linked hands.

"I'm an elemental. We don't experience cold the way the rest of demon-kind do," he rumbled. If only he knew what that deep throaty sound did to me...

Focus, Ruby. Focus.

"You're an elemental?" He nodded. "I didn't know that." He nodded again.

"We keep our powers to ourselves for the most part. If the enemy does not know the extent of what we can do, they err on the side of caution. They are more likely to make very stupid mistakes, much like the imp did with you," he said. I didn't want to think about the imp right now. Not after all the possible sightings I've had these past two weeks. Thinking too much...it made me wonder why he hasn't tried anything. What he was planning. Our kind were not the type to forgive and forget, but instead of saying that, I steered our conversation in a different direction.

"So what elements do you have affinities for? I know about the fire...but I'm guessing that's not the only one." I thought back to the night Josh died and the way Laran had set fire to his body. I shivered again, and not because of the cold. I wasn't afraid of Laran, not anymore at least. We were both capable of truly terrible things.

"I have control over all of the natural elements and their forms."

"Really? How much control?" I asked. I quickly wished I hadn't. Wind swept across the skies, howling like a hound. Clouds rolled in where there previously had been none. Electricity crackled through the air as a single bolt of lightning struck not five feet in front of us.

I stopped dead in my tracks, standing frozen in the middle of the parking lot. My heart pounded in my chest and my eyes went wide as I stole a glance in Laran's direction.

He didn't just have enough control to burn a body.

He could control the very atmosphere.

That type of power was...immeasurable.

If he could summon a storm in seconds, what could he do when he really got angry?

"You can cause natural disasters. That's why you're War," I murmured. The words suspended between us as the pressure dropped. Closing in around us, pulling us together, like magnets. His eyes flashed from black to the darkest of reds. Not brilliant like a rose or a ruby, but still glinting with danger and secrets.

"I have great control over all of them, but I align myself with fire. Maybe that is why I am drawn to you as well." Be still, my beating heart. Laran was not really a sweet talker, but that made his words all the more endearing.

"You Horsemen are much more forward than human men. I'm not sure if I should find it refreshing or concerning," I whispered back. He squeezed my hand gently, but with enough strength to make my skin tingle.

"That's because we're not men. We're demons, and heir to Hell or not—we take what we want. You branded me, Ruby Morningstar. There's no getting rid of me now." His words were a scorching fire against my skin. Words that I reveled in. There was just one thing...

"Do not mistake that brand for love. The beast is possessive. You may like it now, but if you were to be with someone else..." I let my voice trail off as my eyes dropped to his lips. "I can't say for certain, but there is a strong chance I might burn them alive."

"The only reason the human lived as long as he did was because you did not return his affections. Rest assured, Ruby, this brand does not go one way. You may own me, but the only reason I have not branded you is because you share a room with the banshee. For now."

Holy shit.

How the hell could his words turn me on so much when they also kind of scared the shit out of me? Don't get me wrong, I wanted to fuck him seven ways to Sunday.

But branding each other? The beast pushed and shoved, trying to claw her way forward. She wanted that. With all of them.

I wasn't sure if I was ready for that kind of commitment, but I guess I should have thought about that and had a conversation with the bitch inside me before she went and branded him.

Fuck me.

"We should probably get in the car before I do something reckless," Laran whispered. I bit the inside of my cheek to stop myself from leaning forward...

Nope. Nope. Get yourself together, Ruby. Stay strong.

Instead of lunging forward to kiss him, biting his lip, and breaking whatever self-control he held, I rolled back on the balls of my feet and said, "Yeah, we probably should."

I couldn't help but notice the clouds that scattered while I drove to my house in silence. It was a comfortable silence. Not awkward really. I had Laran wait in the living room since he refused to wait in the car while I grabbed the couple of things I needed out of my bedroom: Bandit's pink elephant and hammock, another week's worth of clothes, and the Amaryllis flower I kept in my room. Just because. It would be nice to have a touch of home.

We were in and out in less than fifteen minutes and pulling into the parking garage under their apartment building in another thirty. Would have been half that if not for the traffic.

Laran held the flower pot in one hand and the pink elephant in another as we made our way across the garage. Our footsteps echoed in the silence. The lot was rather empty, but it catered to one of the most expensive high-rises in Portland. The few cars that were down here put my VW to shame. The cheapest one was worth a hundred grand, easily. There weren't tattoo artists living here, that's for damn sure.

"Your firm must make good money for you guys to afford this place," I said as I pushed the button.

"Hmm?" he asked.

"Your firm? Rysten mentioned it the other night," I said absentmindedly as we got in the elevator.

"He told you about Cocks Brothers?" He turned an access key as my hand stilled on the button marked PH. I pressed it once and glanced at him sideways as the doors closed.

"*Cocks* Brothers?" I asked and he stared at me in question. I tossed my head back and roared. "You named yourselves *Cocks* Brothers?"

"Not that kind of cocks," he said defensively. Like I was the one with my mind in the gutter. "Caux. C-a-u-x."

"Like that's any better," I scoffed.

"Allistair's the one that picked it," he grumbled. That got another chuckle out of me.

"Why does that not surprise me?" I said as the doors dinged and slid open.

I took one step outside the elevator when I stopped and stared in awe at the scene playing out before me. Rysten was in the kitchen, desperately trying to protect something. Food. Baked chicken, by the smell of it. Wearing oven mitts, he held a pair of tongs in one hand and a large baking pan that was still giving off little wafts of heat in the other.

That wasn't the part that caught my attention. Not really.

It was that he was holding the pan away from the counter and snapping the tongs as if they were a weapon, trying to deter a certain raccoon standing on the worktop.

"Off! Off with you. No food for the vermin," Rysten scolded, jabbing the tongs in Bandit's direction. Bandit hunched back on his feet and let out a hiss, swiping one of his paws towards the chicken in an attempt to grab it.

Satan save me.

"What are you doing?" I asked them. Both Rysten and Bandit froze mid-fight and slowly their heads turned towards me. Laran stepped out of the elevator beside me and started laughing his ass off.

"What are you laughing at?" Rysten demanded.

"Both of you."

"He's trying to steal all of the fucking food. What do you expect me to do?" Rysten asked. Bandit made a chittering sound, slowly turning around and walking across the counter.

"He's a raccoon, Rysten. What do you expect? Have you been feeding him and giving him plenty of water like I asked you?" I motioned with my hand for Bandit to come to me and he jumped down and ran.

"Yes, I've done everything you asked. He's worse than a bloody hellhound when you're gone," Rysten said. He slowly started to put the chicken back on the counter, watching Bandit like a hawk, expecting him to turn around and make a go for it. I can't say I blamed him. Bandit's done it before.

"Now, Bandit, bud, we've really got to work on your house manners with..." My words left me as I watched him go to Laran and tug on his jeans. Not mine. *Laran's.*

He waited for a whole three seconds as Laran leaned down and offered him his pink elephant. Bandit ignored the elephant and scurried up his arm to perch on his shoulder. Laran stood back up, putting the elephant in the crook of his other arm and scratched Bandit behind the ears.

"What?" Laran asked me.

"Nothing," I said quickly, hurrying into the living room. I've never seen Bandit act that way towards anyone outside of me. Not even Moira. The most he's ever done is tolerate a select few and their presence. That Laran seemed to be growing on him...it gave me hope.

I crossed through the living room, and for the first time, it didn't feel quite so sterile and harsh. Black hairs clung to the expensive white fabric: tale tell signs of Bandit's romping about. As pristine as the white walls, marble floors, and all white furniture color scheme was —I preferred a more lived in look myself.

I walked down the hallway to the left of the fireplace, going to my and Moira's temporary room, sandwiched between Rysten's and Julian's. Inside we had boxes lined against the back-wall of the things we wanted to take with us. Apparently, you can bring possessions to Hell. It just took some finagling to get through all the red tape so the portal keepers would allow it. Who knew?

Perk of having the Horsemen, I suppose.

I tossed my duffel bag on my faded black comforter. Moira's lime green alarm clock read five thirty in bright white numbers. I wondered what time she'd be rolling in. She said she was packing, and that meant she was cleaning as she went, and that by itself could keep her there until seven tonight, but at least she would miss traffic.

"Dinner's ready," Rysten said behind me. I turned and gave him a small smile.

"Lead the way."

When we got back into the kitchen, Laran was leaning on the counter feeding Bandit pieces of chicken off his plate. I smirked at my raccoon, shaking my head.

"Must you feed him from the table?" Rysten asked, whipping us up two plates. Laran ignored him while Rysten set them on the bar and pulled out the middle chair for me.

"Laying it on a little thick, aren't you?" Laran said without looking our way. I choked on a snort and Rysten glared at him, taking his seat on the other side of me.

We ate our dinner in relative silence, since any time either of them tried to speak with me it devolved into slights of hand and petty slurs. At least the food was great. Baked chicken, roasted potatoes, and green beans. I ate two plates before I had to put my dish in the sink and accept surrender.

We migrated towards the couch where the stalemate continued. Laran sat on my left and Rysten on my right, while Bandit ran off with his pink elephant. Probably burrowing it in my sheets for me to find later.

"What do you want to watch on TV?" Rysten asked, flipping through Netflix.

"We could start season two of *How to Get Away with Murder*."

"Alright."

He pressed play and the intro started rolling. Not ten minutes into it, a quiet tension started building between the three of us. I peeked a glance at Rysten, but his eyes were firmly on the TV. When I looked over at Laran, he had his elbow propped up with his chin in the palm of his hand.

Well, maybe it was just me then. I folded my hands in my lap and tried to force my attention on the TV. Nope. Still wasn't working. I only made it another ten minutes before I started fidgeting and shifted in my seat. I brought both feet up and tucked my knees under my chin, wrapping my arms around my legs.

There. Maybe that will fix it. Then I am touching absolutely no one.

Five minutes later...

Ten minutes later…

Fifteen minutes later…

The show was almost to the end and I had no fucking idea what was even going on. Somewhere along the way, both Rysten and Laran had scooted closer. They both were such sneaky bastards about it that I didn't notice.

Ah hell. I stood up from my seat and walked into the kitchen. Under the counter on the far right, they had a wine cooler Rysten had so nicely pointed out. I was going to make use of it.

"What are you doing?" Rysten asked.

"She's clearly pouring herself a glass of wine," Laran mocked. The damn bickering, while funny at times, was beginning to get on my nerves.

"Who said anything about a glass?" I muttered to myself, pulling out a nice bottle of Chardonnay and popping the seal. I dug through three drawers before I found the wine opener.

"Ah-ha," I said under my breath. Popping the cork, I inhaled the sweet scent. I took a small sip straight from the bottle and moaned in delight.

"Enjoying yourself over there?" Laran called. I waved them off and took a much larger gulp. The full-bodied white wine washed over me like an old friend. The zest of fruit and unmistakable sweetness paired with a hint of vanilla was simply excellent.

I wasn't a wine snob, but I could pretend, eh?

"So, what did I miss?" I asked, strolling up around the couch during the credit scene. They eyed me with varying levels of amusement as I clutched the bottle in one hand and plopped down between them. If they were going to test my limits, I could sure as hell return the favor. Especially with my trusty friend here.

"Nothing much. I don't understand what the point of this show is," Laran grumbled.

"What's not to understand? You got Viola Davis over here as our badass lawyer. She's followed around by her team of wannabe lawyers. Meanwhile, they've all killed someone or fucked someone they shouldn't have and need to cover it up. Hence, *How to Get Away with Murder*. It's a high production soap. Don't think too hard." I stopped to take another drink of the Chardonnay. It was quite good.

"And this is what humans spend all their time doing?" he asked incredulously.

"Pretty much, yeah," I said. He held out his hand for the bottle of wine and I debated telling him to get his own. Then again, technically, this was his and I was the one mooching. So there is that. I passed the bottle over. "If you drink it all, you have to go get me another one."

He drank about a third of the bottle in two large gulps. Prick.

Rysten clicked start on the next episode as Laran passed the bottle back. I shifted to lean my head against his shoulder as I kicked my legs up and swung them over Rysten's lap.

The beast purred, much preferring this arrangement. After a moment of brief shock and silence, they settled in. Laran angled his body so that my head fell on his chest while he wrapped an arm around my waist. The sound of his heartbeat lulled me into a temporary calm while Rysten massaged my feet.

Just for this alone I could keep them around. Rysten can cook. Laran gets along with Bandit. Both seem to have a decent idea of what cuddling looks like. Although, if it weren't for there being three of us, I suspect we'd be doing much more interesting things right now than pretending to watch a TV show.

I finished off the bottle of wine only fifteen minutes in, not that it was really me drinking the whole bottle when Laran kept stealing sips and grimacing. He struck me as more of an ale kind of guy. You know, the kind of guy that stands there shirtless while he throws axes and drinks a stein of beer. But who was I to tell a man what to drink?

We watched another episode or two, finally settling into some sort of temporary peace. I knew the jibes were there just under the surface when every now and then a character would say or do something that had Laran either rolling his eyes or scowling while he muttered how utterly stupid they were. Rysten simply smirked and we would share a private glance. He understood the show and what I liked about it. He got me in that way, and it was something that I knew I was going to be eternally grateful for as time went on. Outside Moira, he was the only one.

Moira...

What time was it? And why wasn't she home?

Something wasn't right here.

As the end credits rolled across the screen for the

third episode in a row, I moved my legs off Rysten and onto the marble floor. "I need to use the bathroom," I told them. Not a lie, but it wasn't the whole truth. Laran's arm slipped from my waist as I stood up off the couch and padded down the hall into the side bathroom. In one hand, I still clutched the empty wine bottle as I reached for my cell phone with the other.

It was nearly eight thirty.

And I had no new messages.

Paranoia and panic vied for control as I typed out a message to Moira. It was just a quick, 'Are you ok?' And then I sat down to use the bathroom. I washed my hands in the pretty stone sink and swiped my empty Chardonnay bottle off the floor. *Why did I carry this in here?*

My phone buzzed. It was Moira. She sent a picture.

I swiped left, half expecting a dumb gif revolving around yoga or *Rick and Morty*.

But what I saw...it was my worst nightmare.

Time rolled to a stop. My heart skipped a beat and adrenaline flooded my system as I took in all the details. Moira's bedroom. Her rumpled bedspread. The blue shimmering liquid that matted part of her forest green hair to her face.

Forest green. Her glamor was down.

The dazed look in her eyes. She was alive, but she was strung out.

My phone rang to "Fergilicious." It was a ringtone I knew well.

I swiped right and brought the receiver to my ear.

Praying I was wrong.

Knowing I wasn't.

"Did you get my picture, dollface?" I'd heard this voice before.

I was dumb enough to believe it would stay in my nightmares.

CHAPTER 17

"Yes." My voice was stiff, but steady. I don't know how, but I was thankful it was. Moira wouldn't want me to beg.

"Excellent."

"What do you want?" I asked him. It wasn't a plea, but it was close. I would get on my hands and knees and fucking crawl if that's what he asked.

But he wouldn't.

That wasn't enough for him. Not after that night. After Julian.

"I've given her too much black lotus it seems. You have twenty minutes to come home before she receives a second dose. This one will be fatal. If you tell anyone, I will put a bullet in her brain and be gone before they can catch me."

The bottle slipped from my fingers and shattered on the marble floor as I thought of her dying. Flicks of pain and slices of fire licked at my skin where the glass edges cut me. I didn't give a single damn.

"Time is ticking, Lucifer's daughter."

The phone went dead at the same moment the bathroom door came off the hinges.

Laran and Rysten took in everything from the shattered bottle to my terror-stricken expression. I had two choices: lie through my teeth and run off to be a hero, possibly dying while I was at it...or I could tell them the truth and send the full might of the Four Horsemen to kill him and save her.

"He has Moira," I choked. "He took her."

I knew how these manipulation games worked. He wanted me to ask myself too many questions.

Would he really know whether I told them or not?

Would he actually kill her if I did?

The answer was yes and no.

He would kill her, but he had no fucking way of knowing if I told the Horsemen. He was a single demon. Not an omnipotent entity.

He wouldn't know until it was too late.

Deep down in my heart of hearts, a funeral march was beginning.

He took Moira.

How? I did not know. I could only assume he cornered her somehow and forced those terrible drugs into her.

The hopelessness. The desperation. It all came down on me like a tidal wave intent on holding me under, but I would not succumb. Not yet.

"Ruby, I need you to tell me how you know that?" Laran asked. I held up the phone screen and his face changed color. "She's been drugged."

"He called after he sent this. I have twenty minutes to get home before he gives her a second dose that will kill her. If he sees you coming, he said he will shoot her in the head and be gone before we can catch him." This time my voice shook. Was it despair that had me? Or was it death?

"We're going to get her back, I promise—"

"Don't make promises you can't keep."

"Ruby—"

I pushed past him into the hallway where Allistair and Julian had just arrived. How had they gotten here so fast? You know what—it didn't matter.

"Don't! You know as well as I do he has no intention of letting her live. Whether I go or not." I spat the words like a vile poison and started tugging my boots on over my bloodied feet.

"You're right," Julian said putting a hand on my shoulder. I brushed it off and stormed towards the door, but Allistair grabbed me by the wrist and pulled me back.

"Which is exactly why you aren't going," Allistair supplied.

"What?" I looked between their faces, searching for any indication of why they would possibly do this. "What do you mean *I'm not going*?" I demanded, my voice rising an octave.

"Calm down, love. Think about this—"

"Don't fucking tell me to calm down!" I snapped.

"Moira is not just my best friend. She's my family. If there's even a chance she's going to die, I need to be there." The flames in the fireplace turned blue, bathing us in an unnatural light. Allistair didn't release me, and the Horsemen didn't yield.

"If you go, then our priorities will be to keep you safe. If you love her, then you will stay here while we—" I raised my hand for silence.

"While you go and fight?" I supplied. The bitterness in my tone couldn't be faked, but neither could the hardness in his eyes. He wasn't yielding. Nor would Allistair. Nor Rysten. Not even Laran...although he looked like he understood.

"Yes."

I shook my head, not believing this. I was supposed to be queen. To rule one day. I couldn't even get them to let me go after one single fucking demon that *they* couldn't seem to track down. I did the responsible thing and told them. I wasn't keeping secrets.

And yet...I was beginning to wonder if this was only the beginning of the bars that being Hell's heir would create. To one day rule was to be a prisoner...

And if Moira died...

"Well, let me tell you this, *Death*." I spat his name like it was poison. "I will die if she dies. So you better give everything you have to save her. I don't care what you have to do. I don't care who you have to kill. You understand? I don't care. But if you don't bring her back alive, then don't come back at all, because there will be no one here waiting when you return." It was not the beast speaking, but the Queen. The would-be queen. Never in my life had I made demands of people, but this time...nothing was too great a price for Moira. *Nothing*.

They all watched me with stunned faces as I shook off Allistair and took my seat at the bar. Bandit came running down the hallway and leapt onto my lap, curling protectively around me.

Just like that, they were talking around me again, but no one dared ask my opinion.

I was just the precious fucking heir. Too powerful to be risked.

What a crock of bullshit.

My phone vibrated again and my stomach plummeted.

Please don't tell me he knows...

But it wasn't Moira who texted me.

It was an unknown number. I frowned, hiding the phone behind Bandit as I opened the message.

'You're late for work.'

I stared at the four little words. Late for work? Blue Ruby was closed. I had no clients, and devil knows none of them would say—

Slowly, I typed out, *'Who is this?'*

The reply was instant: *'A friend.'*

A friend, huh? I could message back and forth all day to try to weasel the identity out of them, but Moira doesn't have a day. She doesn't even have half an hour.

I watched the four demons in front of me as they talked strategy on how they would enter the house.

Talked about who was needed, and who would stay. For my protection, of course.

You know what? Fuck them.

'Is my friend at work?'

I waited for the reply. The guys were now speaking in hushed tones between themselves, and I knew it was almost time.

My phone vibrated again.

'Yes.'

Shit. If that meant what I thought it did...

'Thank you.'

I clicked the lock button as the Horsemen broke apart and turned to me. It's been less than five minutes and already so much had changed. We now stood on two sides: me with secrets, and them in the dark.

I had no idea what would await them at home, but my gut told me it wasn't pretty.

"Three of us are going, one will stay behind. Decide," Julian said. If this was a test to see who I cared for most, then they were all fools.

I glanced between them weighing my options, a plan already forming in my mind. I swallowed hard hoping he wouldn't hate me when this was over. Praying I didn't read him wrong.

"Laran stays."

Julian's expression gave away nothing, and while Allistair was mildly jealous, he knew it wouldn't be him I chose. The only one who really took it to heart was Rysten.

The problem with Rysten is he cared for me too much for this. For what I needed.

Laran aligned with fire. With risks. With passion. With fury.

If anyone would listen, he would. If he didn't...I would cross that bridge when I came to it.

"I'm sorry," Rysten said. He looked like he meant it. I said nothing; not even a goodbye as he and Julian walked into the shadows and disappeared.

"Stay safe, little succubus," Allistair murmured. He turned and walked straight through an obscenely large mirror. I thought they had so many because he was vain, but a mirror walker made just as much sense. I filed that information away for later.

My phone buzzed one last time, but I didn't dare check it with Laran watching me so closely. He crossed the living room with sure and steady steps. Coming to stand between my legs as I remained perched on my barstool.

"You didn't choose me because you care more about me or to spite the other three."

"No, I didn't."

He nodded, stuffing his tongue in his cheek.

"Why did you choose me, Ruby?" He didn't say it hard or brash. It was honest; more resigned. Open.

"Because you're War. Because you're smart and you can think about your enemy if you stop thinking about me. So far, none of you have stopped thinking about *me*. Can you honestly tell me that you think this enemy would be so stupid as to tell me where my best friend is at, and even risk me telling you?" I was taking a major gamble here, but he'd yet to shut me down. I waited for a moment while he struggled with his own internal debate.

Eventually he said, "No."

"What would you do?" I asked, trying desperately not to keep checking the time. I needed him to believe me. To believe this. To see that I was smarter and better and stronger than they believed.

To trust me enough to not try to stop me.

He cocked his head for a moment, and for the first time I saw the wheels really turning. "I would set a trap and then I would move her, anticipating that you would tell us. That way, if you didn't, you were eliminated, and if you did, we were. Either way, someone dies. Then I would kill Moira and disappear into the night..." His lips parted as he stared at me. Was it shock? Or was it suspicion? Either way, we were running out of time. "She's not at your house. But you already knew that."

"I also don't think he waited to give her a lethal dose of black lotus. Moira is not a full-demon, Laran, and if he did, she is dying." I was breaking inside. My palms were sweating. My pulse was sprinting. I could barely think, and I didn't dare feel.

"You're right. She's not the real target."

"It isn't me either. It's you. You destroyed him for touching me. Julian killed whatever demons he had left. None of this was ever about me, and it only is now because he knows I'm the way to get to you." He did not flinch or look away, despite the hurt I knew that caused him. He blamed himself for that night so much more than I did, but I would not pull punches where the truth was concerned. Not when Moira's life was at stake. I refused.

"If anything happens to you, I will never forgive myself," he said, but I could see I was wearing him down.

"If anything happens to Moira, I will not be the Ruby you know. I will not give a damn if Hell freezes over and the apocalypse comes." Every word was like an ice pick against his armor. I pounded relentlessly at the bond he and the others had, asking him to do the unthinkable and turn against them. "I'm not asking you to kill me, Laran. I'm asking you to trust me. I am not defenseless and I'm tired of being treated like I am. I get that the world is dangerous, but how do you expect me to ever rule Hell if you do not let me make my own decisions? Moira is dying, and if we don't save her, then you will only have yourselves to blame if I become the beast that you are so hell-bent on having me learn to control."

His jaw tightened and I knew I hit a low blow, but we were out of time. It was now or never.

"Don't make me regret this," he growled.

Oh thank fuck. Now I just hoped we made it in time.

"We need to get to my shop. I think he's holding her..." I started for the elevator door when a swirling vortex of flame appeared before game.

"You can *pyroport*?" I asked, staring into what very well could be a portal to Hell. You'd never know until you crossed it.

"Aye," he breathed, linking my hand in his. "We're

only going to have a fraction of a second before he real-izes we're there. Your job is to handle Moira. Do not engage with him unless you're forced. We don't know how many will be there. Do you understand?"

I nodded, staring into the flames. Not so long ago, I was afraid of men and demons. I went out of my way to avoid them and keep my head down for the most part. Sure, I played with fire on occasion, but I always knew I was going to get burned.

For the first time in my life, I was willingly staring into the face of danger and I could truthfully say I was unafraid of it. Fire bathed my face, but I stared back at it ready for what I would find.

I was a friend of death, and a queen of demons, and a slayer of men.

I was a girl on fire, and the flames only answered to me.

JULIAN

She hated me.

More than any of the others, she hated me. But we couldn't let her go.

She didn't have a firm grasp on her abilities. Ruby was just as likely to kill the banshee as she was to save her, particularly this close to the transition.

She was a keg of gun powder waiting for a single spark.

When she goes off...

I hung my head because it didn't matter what happened tonight. I had failed her. She was my queen, and I made her my prisoner.

But I simply couldn't do it. Even if Moira dies and Ruby never forgives me...at least she's alive.

"It'll be okay, mate. She'll get over it." Rysten clapped me on the back. I bared my teeth and shook him off.

"No, brother, she won't. She'll forgive you because you're as bad as the fucking humans. But I don't think she'll forgive

me," I mentally spat at him. We'd shadow walked to a house down the street from hers and clung to the darkness as we skipped down the row.

It was unnaturally quiet, like the calm before the storm. The pressure in the air was charged for a fight as we stepped into her front yard.

The shattered windows were boarded up, but no light peaked through. Not a single sign of life.

"Can you hear anything?" I asked Rysten. He paused and cocked his head.

"No heartbeat. Only her alarm clock ticking," he replied. I grit my teeth, clenching me jaw.

I was to go in first, through the front door, while Rysten entered the back, and Allistair kept watch outside.

"Allistair."

"I'm in place." he responded instantly. We could not see him, but that was the idea.

If we couldn't see him, neither could anyone else.

"I'm going in," I told them both. Rysten stepped back into the shadows, repositioning himself beside the back door.

"Three."

I crossed the yard in four bounds.

"Two."

I jumped onto the porch, landing about as light and soundless as a gunshot.

"One."

My boot connected with the door, kicking it clean off

the hinges. I stormed into the house headed for the bedroom when I heard something.

"Julian! Julian, it's not an alarm clock, it's a—"

"Bomb," I finished.

Bam!

My skin shriveled and died as the layers were torn to shreds, fire burning and ravaging. Tendons and ligaments stretched and snapped as the impact shattered every bone in my body. I didn't have time to cry out or register the pain. Waiting for my body to repair itself, I focused on my remaining consciousness as my body was ripped apart at the seams. I could hear the echoed voices of my brothers in arms.

"He's down, and I can't reach War."

"What do you mean? Where the fuck is Ruby?"

"This whole thing was a trap. Where the fuck are they?"

I faded into the void where all souls go to cross over. If I were anything less than Death, I would be dead, but I was more than a human or a demon.

I was a god.

Immortal.

Filled with a wrath so cold, it burned.

He planted a bomb meant for Ruby.

Someone was going to pay in blood.

I flexed my fingers and opened my eyes.

The only thing more permanent and guaranteed than my immortality was how quickly I would end his life once I found him.

CHAPTER 18

We stepped through the portal together and appeared inside my office. In only a fraction of a second, the portal was closed, but to our dismay—my office door was not.

From this angle, all you could see was the wall of the cubicle, and while it was silent, we were not alone. A slow clapping began. I looked to the doorway, but the sound wasn't coming from there. Nor was it behind us. The clapping echoed around and within, and from above, but below. It was everywhere, and that's when I knew I was in trouble.

I turned for Laran, but he was nowhere to be seen. It was like he disappeared.

But that can't be true.

Can it?

"I'm so happy you decided to show up, dollface. I didn't think you would figure it out, but pleasant surprises are *always* welcome." The demons voice echoed through my mind.

That couldn't be right. There wasn't an echo in here. This didn't make sense.

I took a hesitant step towards the door and maniacal laughter ensued.

Somehow his voice was blocking everything out. I could hear nothing but him, despite being certain Laran was still with me. He would never abandon me...but I couldn't see him.

Where had he gone?

I took another three steps towards the door when the room turned upside down. The floor was now the ceiling, but I was still standing on the floor. I turned in circles, when a touch ghosted against my back. I jumped and turned, but no one was there.

"Looking for me?" I whirled around to see the imp standing right behind me.

He wore a suit that fit well, and I instantly deemed it pretentious enough that Allistair would wear it. The jacket was navy blue with a white button up. Personally, I think it clashed with his eyes—

He doesn't have two eyes. He only has one.

So why were two watching me?

This made no sense. But then, that was the only part that made sense.

"This isn't real," I whispered. He smiled, and it was almost kind. Almost handsome.

"Very smart, dollface. My mother was not an imp,

but a nightmare. She gave me some very useful gifts for making people pliant. Let's see how strong your mind is, shall we?" The smile dropped from his face as the ground dropped out from beneath me. I fell into free fall and appeared in a room that I wished I had forgotten.

My legs dangled uselessly at the end of the conference table. I struggled to move, to scream, to yell. No one came. Not as Josh dry humped my body or licked my breasts. Not as he undid my jeans and slowly started tugging them down.

Any second now...

Josh whipped them free from my legs. When this happened, I was able to retreat into my mind. That was not an option this time. I was stuck in my worst nightmare. Unable to wake up. Nowhere to flee.

Oh God, don't do this. Don't let this happen. What the fuck did I do to deserve...

Nothing. I did nothing to deserve this.

The first inkling of heat touched me, but it wasn't enough to break free.

It's not real. It's not real. It's not real. I chanted to myself over and over again. Maybe the guys wouldn't come, and maybe I was trapped inside some kind of nightmare, but that didn't make it real.

Just because I had to relive it didn't give it power over me.

As soon as the thought occurred to me, the memory shattered like glass. Breaking apart into a kaleidoscope of images that made up my history.

I fell deeper into the shards of my past and recoiled in horror when I landed.

Josh was terrible. I wished him dead. But this...

This was the real start of it all.

His name was Danny, and he was my first love. At least I thought he was.

We met here in Portland. He was reassigned to the orphanage I lived at. I was fifteen when we first met. Barely more than child, and definitely not a woman. We became fast friends, him and I. Even Moira liked him, which was a first. She literally liked no one but me.

And no one else since.

We knew each other six months before we went on our first date. He took me to Olive Garden. I spilled soup on myself, and because I was too self-conscious to go to the movies after that, we went back to the house and stargazed on the trampoline instead.

Six more months passed, but Danny changed...he grew more demanding in how much time I spent with him. He became insufferable after we had sex. He didn't like that I spent so much time with Moira and tried to get rid of her.

Of course, it was that night I revisited in this nightmare.

My footsteps creaked as I closed the door and crawled into bed. Moira was already out cold for the night. It was unusual, given she had trouble sleeping.

I pulled the thin blanket up over my chest and found myself lulled to sleep faster than normal. I woke, what felt like only minutes later, but when I did, I realized I was not alone.

I opened my mouth to scream as a rag was shoved in it, blocking my cry, constricting my airway. Horror racked my body as I realized who was in bed with me, and what he was doing.

He only used a mild sleeping sedative, thinking that would be enough. He didn't realize the fight I would put up when he got into bed.

Then again, I'm not sure that he was in his sane mind that night, or the months leading up to it.

I lashed out with everything I had, and I mean everything. My body was not strong enough to fight him and get away. I did not know about the beast. I did not have access to fire.

But I had something else.

I latched onto his mind and shredded it like paper.

It was the only thing I could do. I didn't see another way. Hell, I didn't even know I could do it…until I did.

I was so terrified, so hurt, so broken, that I lashed out and drove him mad. Of course, when he realized that I was causing it, he tried to pull away. He tried to run.

He didn't even make it three steps before he collapsed.

I wasn't going to let him get away.

He started babbling about how my touch drove him mad. He didn't consider what my mind could do.

But I was born with a unique ability so terrifying, I forced myself to forget it.

To forget what I did to him.

To forget what I am.

I didn't just shred his mind. I ripped apart his soul, and I didn't even need to touch him to do it.

Moira had awoken. She told me that I called to her. That I needed her. That he was hurting me.

She found him screaming and bashed his head in with a paperweight, leaving him bleeding, his eyes as wide and vacant as a doll.

She found me curled up in a ball. When she hugged me, it hurt less. When she helped me get rid of the body, she made it go away. When she cleaned the blood stain off the wood floors, she became my anchor.

I was drowning in the pain of that night and what I'd done. Because I remembered all of it now. Someone ripped the blinders from my eyes and made me remember what happened.

Remember that I killed his soul.

That Moira broke his body.

And we became sisters tied together by blood.

Once upon a time this memory had the power to break me.

So I forgot it.

Now, I remembered.

And the demon that had forced me to relive this underestimated how much I'd healed since then.

How much stronger I had become.

I couldn't find my flames in here, in this nightmare he created.

But he gave me an even deadlier weapon. And he couldn't take it back.

Mentally I reached out, searching for the very real essence that was all around me. Instinctively, he shied away. Running from the power. He only just realized his mistake.

I knew the moment he withdrew from my mind, because I found myself on my knees before him as he backed away towards the door.

A single eye stared back at me and I smiled, dark and lovely.

"You should have killed us when you had the chance," I said, but I did not give him another one.

He opened his mouth prepared to scream, but the time for screaming was over.

I ripped into him, rage fueling an immeasurable force, devouring his very soul.

Fire sprang to life at my beck and call, breaking his body apart until it was nothing more than glittering ash, dancing in the flames.

I waded through the fire, to the room beyond where I could hear Moira's heartbeat slowing as the drugs took effect in her veins. He was liar and I was killer, but I refused to let Moira be the consequence.

I refused to let her die.

"Ruby!"

I did not turn to the voice as I approached the chair where the demon strapped her down. It was a chair I knew well. I'd tattooed countless people in it.

Flames licked at the ropes, breaking them apart. Her unconscious body slumped over and I lunged forward to catch her. The beast slipping into place. She cradled my best friend as we picked her up and sank to the floor.

Flames brushed over Moira's skin, but it did not burn or char.

Moira was immune to my flames.

"You're going to hurt her. I need Ruby back," Laran called, appearing above us. He was a sight to behold, bathed in a world of only fire. Like Moira, the flames did not seek to harm him.

"She is dying. I will save her because she is our tether. Ours to protect," the beast said in that same lifeless voice. She used my hands to cradle Moira's head with such care.

Moira's skin was so pale that it didn't even look green, only a sickly ash color that pained me to see on her. Her entire body was limp. The heartbeat in her chest fighting to keep pumping despite the drugs weighing it down.

This was Moira.

My Moira.

And she was going to live one way or another.

A brilliant blue light poured from my hands and into her temples. The fire worked quickly as it raced through her blood, burning the chemicals that threatened her life.

Maybe it was a blessing she was asleep for this because this kind of cleansing would not be easy. It was one thing to be immune to the flames, and another to be burned from the inside out. Still, the beast continued to pour fire into her veins until she started to scream.

If she was strong enough to scream, then she was

strong enough to live. Then, and only then, did the fire die out. I saw Moira's eyes staring up into mine. No longer green, but cobalt blue marked with an upside-down pentagram that ran through her pupil and ringed in black.

"I marked you," I whispered.

And then I fainted.

LARAN

She consumed the world in fire.

The flames of Hell raged at her command, incinerating everything she loved and held dear. Enslaved by her fury, and there was no possible way she could control them.

I was locked in my worst nightmare, so sure she was going to die. So sure that I had made the greatest mistake of my existence.

Then the scene shattered, and before me was not just Ruby or her beast, but an avenging goddess.

She struck him dead with a force from her mind that could not, and would not, be contained.

It was a force unlike any other, and for the first time, I wondered which half of her was stronger. The succubus girl that risked everything for her friend, or the beast that let flames loose upon this world.

I did not know, but this was going to change everything.

She was no longer just Lucifer's daughter, Hell's heir, or even a queen to-be.

She was my mate.

"Ruby!" I yelled, chasing after her through the flames. They did not burn me, but I could thank Lucifer for that. The banshee would not have the same immunity. If she killed her like this...it would break her. I did not doubt, not even for a second, that she meant what she said.

If the banshee died, she would not be the same, and both worlds would crumble.

I dived through the fire, unprepared for what I saw.

Ruby sat on her knees holding a half-demon who should not be alive.

No, not Ruby. The beast.

Her eyes were black as sin, void of any emotion.

Only pure obsidian gemstones that belonged to the creature who branded me.

"You're going to hurt her. I need Ruby back," I called. At first, I didn't think she heard me. How could she above the roaring of the flames?

But then she spoke.

"She is dying. I will save her because she is our tether. Ours to protect."

She is our tether...

How did we not see this? The bansh—Moira wasn't just a friend or family. She was Ruby's *familiar*.

This was the reason Ruby could hold off the transition. The reason we had no idea how strong she was. The reason Moira could withstand the flames...was because Ruby physically could not hurt her in any capacity.

Moira had taken on the role of the Horsemen and funneled the power because we had not been here. We just never realized it.

We had completely and utterly failed her before this night.

I fell to my knees before her, keeping my mouth shut.

The signs were all there and we never saw it.

Maybe it was time to watch and listen.

The beast laid her hands on the banshee's face. The smaller girl's normally spring colored skin was sickly and pale. Ruby had been right about that, too. The imp never waited, but I was not dumb or optimistic enough to think he would.

Blue fire spread from her fingertips, flaring to life beneath Moira's skin. It spread like plumes of smoke, lighting up every inch of her body until she glowed so bright that it physically hurt to watch, but I would not look away.

The banshee let out a scream as her eyes flew open. The flames receded instantly.

"I marked you," Ruby whispered.

I threw my arms out and caught her as she fainted.

Blue Ruby Ink was gone. Standing amongst the piles of ash were the Horsemen.

Watching Ruby and Moira with the same grim realization as I.

The world would come for both of them, and if anything happened to Moira...

Ruby would burn anything and everything to the ground.

Our job just got infinitely more complicated.

CHAPTER 19

I woke to the faint whisper of wind as it brushed across my face. Cool. Gentle. I blinked once, taking in the darkness. After floating through a suspended void, I couldn't really call my room at the apartment darkness. Moonlight bathed the boxes aligned on the far wall and shimmering white drapes stirred from a gentle breeze. Someone left the door open to the balcony.

My legs were stiff and unwieldy as I slid them over the black bed sheets and onto the soft carpet. I crinkled my toes, wrapping them around the fibers beneath.

How long was out? How long had passed?

Reaching for my robe sprawled across the comforter, I shrugged it on. I glanced back to the bed where Moira slept soundly. With her eyes closed, I could pretend that it didn't happen. She looked much the same as normal, apart from Bandit being wrapped around her. He clung to her shirt with one paw and wrapped the other around his pink elephant. His face was pushed up over her flat stomach, using her like a pillow. He definitely drooled on her enough for one.

I smiled because they were safe. Inside, my heart was heavy with what would come in the morning. Was Laran alright? Were the others? Someone had to have brought us back here. Those were questions for the morning.

My legs protested as I rose from the bed and took shaky steps across the bedroom to the open doors. The flames of Hell were not nearly as physically exhausting as my other ability.

Soul-shredding, was it?

Something along those lines. I could ask Moira in the morning.

I reached out and grasped my hand around the edge of one of the balcony doors, using it to stabilize me while I crossed over the threshold and out into the night. My toes tingled against the cold stone. I wrapped my arms around myself, drawing the bathrobe tight. Not that it did much in this weather.

Twenty-three stories up in the dead of night...the view was breathtaking. Skyscrapers towered high around the city, but none so tall from where I was at. They lit up in shades of gold, blue, and green against a dark, starless sky. I truly felt small.

I drew in a deep breath, knowing I was not alone.

I knew she was there in the shadows where I could not see.

She'd been following me for some time now, after all.

"You know, some thought I was crazy for wanting to leave the south and live here. They called me a child because I saw the picture on a post card once and made it my mission to move. Far enough north to hide from most of demon-kind, but in a city of marvels so that I always had inspiration." My voice was hardly a whisper on the wind, but I knew she heard me.

"It's a great view. I'll give you that," she said quietly. The wind carried her words to my ears, as I gripped the stone ledge of the balcony.

"Why did you help me?" I asked, still not looking her way. She wouldn't kill me. If she wanted to do that, she would have let Moira die.

"Which time?" she replied.

The pressure shifted as her presence drew closer. I could sense brutal power and pain coming from it, but also...resistance. Where my own inner light was blue, this light was distinctly darker. A shade of indigo.

Startled, I realized that was her soul.

This was going to take some getting used to...

"You told me where to find her. How did you know I would listen?"

"I didn't, but I suspected."

"You suspected?"

"You knew someone was looking out for you, but in the end, it was your choice," she said.

"And the Seelie?" I continued, still staring at the skyline. I was going to learn to treasure these sights because they would be gone from my life very soon.

"I wish I could say it was out of the goodness of my heart, but it wasn't." She breathed out a very tired sigh. "You're the next ruler of Hell, and that makes you a very powerful person. A threat to my master. I was sent to take out the rogue demon, and to watch you, even kill you if I had the chance."

So the legions of Hell had arrived. The Horsemen weren't kidding.

Powerful people wanted me dead, and now, they knew where to find me.

"But you didn't," I said, drawing my eyes away from the view. She stood no more than three feet from me, almost exactly as I remembered her; the exception was a dark cloak, obscuring most of her body. Her snow-white hair reflected silver in the moonlight. She had it pulled back in a braid, the purple ends hidden from sight. The darkness made her mercury colored eyes more vivid and striking.

"No," she whispered. "I didn't."

"Why? I kicked you out of my house. I threatened you. You didn't even have to do it yourself, and I probably would have died...but you saved me. Why?" We stared at each other suspended in time. The wind did not move, nor did the sky. Not a single living being stirred, even those only feet from us.

"Because I was watching when the mob came to your shop and I saw what you did when they threw rocks at your family. I watched you, and I saw good. I saw a future for Hell that wouldn't be marked by blood wars and senseless killing." She averted her eyes to the heavens, but there would be no God that looked down on us this night. An assassin and a killer. Two demons entering something unholy and yet divine. "You have not been around long enough to see the things I have. The horrors our kind must either become or endure. You are not like the rest of us, not completely. You, Lucifer's daughter, can change the future of Hell. But more importantly to me—you can change my future."

A loose strand of white and purple hair slipped free from her braid, blowing in the wind. I wasn't sure if I should be thankful for what she did, anxious about the supposed future she saw, or concerned because now we had gotten to the heart of the matter.

"You want something from me."

"Yes," she replied. "Not right now, but later. Call it a favor for investing in your future."

"And yours," I said tersely. Her eyes narrowed as she watched me, debating if she made the right choice trusting me. I didn't fault her for it, just as I didn't fault her for expecting something in return. That was just how the world was; an exchanging of goods and favors. It's how empires were built, and queens were made.

I would do right to remember that.

People always said the road to Hell was paved with good intentions, but no one's intentions are ever actually good. We all are a little selfish. More than a little for most of us. I couldn't trust someone who walks with good intentions, but I could bargain with someone who had honest ones. The path to living wouldn't come without a price. This was hers.

"I owe you, and should I actually live long enough to rule—whatever that entails—well, you know how to find me." She relaxed just a fraction before whipping out one claw-tipped hand and swiping at me. I jumped back, hitting my back against the stone balcony, and my weak legs wobbled from over-exhaustion.

"What was that—"

I watched as she dragged the same claw across her own skin, my blood mixing with hers. A sizzling sensation spread across my left breast where she'd cut me. I pulled the fabric aside, to see a very thin but already cauterized scar.

"Blood magic," I whispered. I didn't dare say more.

"Consider it insurance that you make good on your word," she replied.

I swallowed hard and nodded. There was no point challenging something that can't be undone.

The she-demon turned away and I knew our meeting was coming to an end.

"Wait," I called. She paused and tilted her chin to the side.

"The text messages you sent me—they were written in code. Why?"

She smiled, like she was pleased with me. Certainly not surprised. "We are being watched, you and I. There are more coming."

"Who's watching?" I asked. There was no point in asking who was coming. The Horsemen had already warned me of this. Demons. From all over the world. The demon from the Black Brothers had known who I was, and I would bet my life savings he made sure the rest of the world knew it, too.

"I can't say."

"Is it your master?"

Again, she smiled. I was starting to get the hang of this. She could intervene, but only so far. I had to work for the answers I needed.

"There are powerful people in play. Trust no one, not even me, if you want to live long enough to see yourself on the throne. Evil doesn't just hide in the shadows." Her parting words made me shiver, and in the blink of an eye, she was gone.

I didn't bother searching up and down for her. She would turn up again when she wanted to be found, and not a minute before.

The first rays of a new dawn broke the cusp of the skyline as I returned to bed, only then realizing that I didn't even know her name.

CHAPTER 20

It was all over the news the next morning. A fire burned down the entire strip Blue Ruby Ink was in. The kitchen on the other side of us had a wood oven. Press said someone didn't shut the chamber and the fire spread. The restaurant's furnace cracked and fire shot down the lines of the building, leveling everything in its path.

It was a freak accident, but luckily not a tragedy.

No one died. No one human, anyways.

I tugged my hood forward as I stood across the street from my old life. Blue Ruby Ink was gone. My house was gone. Ashes blew in the wind and mixed with the rain, coating the street before me in a black glittery sludge. Cold seeped through my thin jacket, burning my lungs with every breath, giving me the clarity to look at the scene before me and see it for what it was.

The last nail in the old me's coffin.

Was it fitting my fire would be the thing that took the

place I loved away from me? It was certainly ironic. My life goes up in ashes, and from it I rise again.

That sounds nice, right? Motivational? Inspirational?

"What are you thinking about?" Moira asked. I tore my eyes away from the dreary, fucked up mess before me.

"That I'm tired of running from whatever comes next," I said. She grinned up at me, and the pentagrams in her cobalt eyes swirled like smoke.

"I guess that makes two of us. Do you want to ask the lazy fucks if they want a ride to Martha's, or make them work for their forgiveness?"

I grinned back at her, happy to see that at least some things don't change.

"I should probably offer. Try to smooth things over with them," I said begrudgingly. We walked a few yards down the sidewalk where Rysten and Julian waited. They'd tried to give me space since I woke up, but I didn't know if it was for me, or for them.

I suppose only time would tell how long it took to repair the trust on both sides. Moira would have died. So I didn't regret or even apologize for what I did. No matter how many I'm-sorry, but-please-never-do-that-again hugs Rysten tried to give me, or broken stares that Julian thought I didn't see. They could be sorry all they wanted, but it wouldn't make a damn difference. I wasn't changing, and if they thought I was going to let them make all my choices for me after we left...they had another thing coming.

"Would you like to ride with us? I want to get break-fast at Martha's before we leave," I asked them.

"That would be nice. Thank you, love," Rysten said, offering me his arm as I linked mine through it. I looked at Julian as I held out my other hand. He froze for a moment, until I turned it over and opened it. "You can drive."

Julian looked at the keys and a wiry smile came to his lips. He took them from me and strode ahead. A little more umph in his step. It would take time for us to fix this between us, but olive branches went a long way at bridging the gap.

"I call shot gun!" Moira said, stomping right after him. Yes, some things never change.

"I'm not sure what to think of this," Rysten muttered.

"Think of what?" I asked.

"You branded War *and* the banshee before me," he said. "And here I thought I was your favorite."

I chuckled under my breath as we sidled up to the car.

"I was saving Moira's life. You can't exactly be jealous about that," I said, fighting the smile that Rysten still seemed to be able to pull out of me. Even after all this.

"Just promise me something," he whispered in my ear.

"Mmmm?" I leaned in, grinning into the crook of his shoulder.

"I'm next," he growled. If my lady parts didn't just light up...I shivered into the soft caress of his lips. Oh yes, the beast was more than happy to make him next.

Filthy slut.

"Ahem," Moira coughed. I caught her arched eyebrow over Rysten's shoulder and started to pull away.

"Earn it," I whispered back to him. He chuckled under his breath and let me go. We drove to the diner in relative silence, or at least as much silence as could be expected when Moira was in the car and giving Julian driving tips.

Meanwhile, my mind wandered.

We had to leave Portland for obvious reasons and couldn't go to Hell just yet. Allistair would stay behind and get my home and business insurance settled, and then begin the process of getting all my shit moved across worlds. What was left of it, anyways.

Not to mention the questions being asked about the convenience of both my house and my tattoo parlor blowing up the same night. No allegations had been brought to the table, but Allistair would sort them out.

At the end of the day, it was mostly a ruse. He was sticking around to keep his ear to the ground. Trouble was coming, and I would be long gone by the end of the hour.

But I did want my things.

They still hadn't told us where we were going yet. All I got this morning were vague answers about Laran getting everything 'squared away.'

We pulled into Martha's Diner and my eyes pricked with moisture as I got out of the car. The door jingled the same as it always did when we walked in and we took my usual table. Kendall and her cronies were nowhere to be found and I suspected she wouldn't be for a good long while.

I slid into the booth and Rysten followed suit, with Julian and Moira taking a seat across from us.

"What will it be for you this morning, Ruby?" Martha asked, coming to us from behind the counter. She smiled without reservation. Good, she hadn't heard the news. That will make at least this goodbye easier.

"Four plates of bacon and black coffee."

"I don't know why I even ask."

It was the same conversation we had for ten years. I was going to miss the ease, but even now, it no longer felt quite so simple. When breakfast was over, it would be time for me to go.

"It's going to be okay, love," Rysten leaned in and whispered as everyone placed their order. That was all any of us said that even hinted at what's to come. The rest of breakfast was filled with Rysten's dry wit, typically at Julian's expense, while Moira and I laughed along.

When Martha brought the check out and wished me a happy Saturday, I smiled and wished her one as well. She would never know what happened to me, and I couldn't tell her. No one could know we were leaving, but I suppose the tip I left her would probably be a hint. I was the last to walk out of the diner and would not be there when she noticed that I had left my life savings and car keys on the table.

Granted, it wasn't much, but they were all I had to give to the woman that watched me from afar these past years and gave me a safe place to go. Eventually she would see the news, but maybe now she would know I was alright.

As we walked down an alley, the clouds opened, casting down a single ray of sunshine. I thought it was odd…then I realized what it was spotlighting. Or who, rather.

"Hi there, stranger," I called.

Laran saddled up to my side, Bandit riding perched on his shoulder.

"Alright, you've been holding out on us long enough. Where are we going?" Moira demanded, putting her hands on her hips. Apparently, I was the only one that believed in any kind of common courtesy around here.

"What is this about me holding out on you?" he asked me, completely ignoring Moira. She narrowed her eyes at him and I could practically see the wheels turning.

"Do I need to scream to—"

Before I could speak, a portal of fire appeared before me and someone pushed me through. I screamed for all of two seconds before landing with a thump on something soft.

What the fuck did he—

"MOTHERFUCKKKKKEEEEEEERRRRRR!"

Thunk!

I rolled over in the bed to see Moira sitting next to me, wide-eyed and pissed off.

"That asshole just pushed me through a portal," she cursed.

"Yes, well. Rest assured, we thought it was quite amusing," Rysten said, stepping out of the shadows.

"Allistair told me how much you loved being pushed off things," Laran laughed, appearing through a ring of fire.

"I might actually kill you," I spat, leaping from the bed to tackle him. Bandit jumped from his shoulder to protect himself and started making this awful choking sound. If I didn't know any better, I would say he was fucking *laughing*.

"Now, Ruby, are you sure you want to do that? Look outside," Rysten said right as I barreled into Laran, and to my credit, slammed him into a wall.

What the—

"Did that actually just happen?" Moira screeched. "Like, she really just *body slammed* War—"

"Ruby, love. Why don't you come here for a second?" Rysten asked, his pleasant tone coated in concern.

I stood still, shocked, both hands pressed on Laran's chest, trying to discern why my head was *so* hot.

I mean, it was burning.

I could barely even think—

"War, are you physically able to move?" Julian asked behind me. His voice was cool and calculated, emanating power.

Laran tensed against my hands, but didn't move a single inch. I pushed against him, harder this time. A crack ran through the house as he fell through the wall, landing in a heap of drywall and dust on the other side.

"Well that answers that," Julian noted.

"What the fuck just happened?" I asked, snapping out of it and pulling away.

"Well, love. It appears that you're entering the transition. You won't have more than forty-eight hours before it goes into full effect," Rysten said calmly. He approached me with his hands raised in surrender.

"Why are you acting like that?" I shouted, storming out of the room even though I had no idea where the fuck I was. Laran just pushed me through a damned portal and then—

I closed my eyes and cursed, taking in deep breaths.

In the background, I could hear the guys debating back and forth. Something about Julian needing to man up and my impeccable timing. I opened my eyes and blinked. The emotions cleared just long enough for me to take in my surroundings. The fuzzy white carpet and black leather furniture. The startling glass wall in front of me, reflecting sunshine off the dust particles in the air.

The cityscape that every single demon child on the North American continent is taught to recognize.

New Orleans.

The city of the dead.

Also known as Hell's gates.

Fuck me.

To be continued...

Text "Books" to (844) 506-1510
To stay up to date on future releases and sales!
If you loved this book and want to connect more with Kel

and her other readers, please join her Facebook Readers Group at https://www.facebook.com/groups/thecrowsnestreadersguild for more shenanigans!

Continue the series with:
Infernal Desires
Queen of the Damned
Book 3

ABOUT THE AUTHOR

Kel Carpenter is a master of werdz. When she's not reading or writing, she's traveling the world, lovingly pestering her editor, and spending time with her husband and fur-babies. She is always on the search for good tacos and the best pizza. She resides in Maryland and desperately tries to avoid the traffic.

Join Kel's Readers Group!

Acknowledgments

Some stories are difficult, and some are easy. Wicked Games was a book that wrote itself, and after several edits and revisions, I still love to read it. That said, managing school and writing while also preparing for this release has been more than a little stressful. To Analisa, my friend and editor who puts up with my shit and makes these books readable, thanks hun. I probably owe you more than one bottle of scotch at this point. To Carrie and Courtney, your combined moral support and shenanigans have helped more than you know. I love you, bitches. To Matt, I should probably be thanking you the most for forcibly removing the cats when they decided to lay on my computer while I was editing. Without you, this probably wouldn't have been ready in time.

And finally, to the readers that have read these books and inundated me with raccoon videos: you guys are awesome. Thank you for supporting me as an author. Also, please look up your state laws before trying to adopt one.